New Beginnings

To order additional copies, please contact us.
BookSurge, LLC
www.booksurge.com
1-866-308-6235
orders@booksurge.com

LaVERNE
CASH

NEW
BEGINNINGS

A HOGAN'S HEROES STORY

2004

May the Lord bless and keep you and bring you home safe

LaVerne Cash
Phil 4:13

New Beginnings

CONTENTS

ACKNOWLEDGMENTS

Reverend Ken Tipton - for providing the inspiration for Private Ken Tiptoe and tons of material for him, also for 20 years of laughter, music, prayers, inspiration, Living Christmas Trees, and driving me crazy. Did I mention *LAVERNE?*

Mr. Jeff Smart (historian for the US Army Research Development and Engineering Command) — for providing me with two excellent references on the history of biological warfare.

A very special thanks to

Mrs. Mel Hughes — for encouraging me to write this, providing me with historical and cultural information and for letting me borrow characters and situations she created.

Ms. Eva Seifeit for writing the *Theather of War* series, which started my mind to working.

Ms. Kathrine Rend - for all her hard work on the cover design.

Mrs. Linda Groundwater for editorial assistance

In honor and memory of all the talented individuals both in front of and behind the cameras who made Hogan's Heroes the wonderful classic that it is today.

To Mel Hughes and Eva Seifeit who encouraged the writting of and also contributed material to this book.

Finally, to those past and present who serve in the armed forces. May your contributions to the cause of freedom never be forgotten.

THE STORY BEHIND THE STORY

*I*n the beginning was "Theater of War" and LaVerne saw that it was good...

The story behind how *New Beginnings* came to be is nearly as convoluted as the story itself. One day I was surfing the net and decided to check out what was on TV that night. I discovered TVLAND was showing reruns of the old *Hogan's Heroes* series. Having been a fan since the original run, and not having seen it in years, I was thrilled to see it back on the air. I then decided to check out some of the links to *Hogan's Heroes* websites. One contained an excerpt from *Theater of War* by Eva Seifeit. Fan fiction is something I don't normally care too much about because a lot of it is fantasizing on the part of the author, inconsistent with the original, lacks depth, and sometimes gets a little weird. This particular excerpt was different. It was well written, had an intriguing story line and got my attention. Even so, I was determined not to buy the book simply because I just didn't want to get into all that fanomanic stuff. On my own, I came up with several variations of the direction I thought the story might take. Finally curiosity got the better of me. In desperation to find out how the story really ended, I broke down and ordered a copy of *Act One*. I enjoyed *Act One* so much that I ordered *Act Two* and *Act Three*. After reading all three, I ask to be put on Eva's mailing list for future books and I emailed her comments on the books. During our discussions,

I questioned some of her background on Hogan. Eva informed me a friend was writing a prequel that might answer some of those questions. Later, when I received Eva's notification that Mel had finished *Dress Rehearsal*, I didn't think twice. I ordered it simply because I trusted Eva's judgment. I was right to do so. I enjoyed *Dress Rehearsal* just as much as I had Eva's books. As I had with Eva, I also sent Mel comments on her book.

At this point let me digress a moment to say I'm a scientist and therefore have an analytical mind. I'm a stickler about logic, consistency, and thoroughness. Since Mel's book, Eva's books, and the series were all intertwined, I examined them all very thoroughly for consistency, holes, and analyzed the plots. I then wrote a 12-page essay on my findings and sent it to both authors. As a result, Mel and I began communicating on a regular basis.

One day during a discussion Mel said, "Hey, you've got some good ideas there. You should try writing them up." To which I came up with a thousand reasons why I couldn't. "I can't spell. I can't type. My writing mechanics are lousy. I'm a technical writer not a fictional writer. I don't have time." Not knowing what she was getting herself into, Mel offered to help me with the writing mechanics and editing. Still, I wasn't quite sold on the idea. It's easy to be a critic; it is something else entirely to be creative. I wasn't sure I could create a story that would stand up to my own scrutiny.

Sometime later a personality issue relating to Hogan came up. Both Mel and Eva felt Hogan operated off the seat of his pants. My reaction was "You've never worked for Ken Tipton." To put that remark in context let me digress again to explain. Ken Tipton is the minister of music at my church, and he is also the poster child for seat-of-the-pants operations. It is not unusual for him to call a soloist at, oh say, 3:00 on a Sunday afternoon to ask that individual to sing at 6:00 the same night (that's considered advance notice). I happen to be one of several sound operators for the church who has to deal with his spur-of-the-moment style of planning. One Easter Sunday Ken planned to have the choir sing with the orchestra. Easter being my turn to run sound and knowing Ken's plans solely from being in the choir myself, I came in on Saturday to set up the system. Lo and behold the floral committee had put flowers all over the front where the orchestra normally sits. I had no clue as to where the orchestra was going to be, so I had no clue as where to set up mikes. In a panic I called Ken at home and asked him if he had seen the platform.

"I know, the floral committee told me what they were doing. I don't have a problem with it."

"Well, then where do you plan to put the orchestra?" *When did you plan to tell me, five minutes before the service started?*

"Oh, on the front row of the choir."

"Ken, you can't do that, the choir mikes hang right over the front row. The orchestra will drown out the choir."

"Well, the orchestra doesn't need to be miked."

"It does matter, the choir needs to be miked. The orchestra will still come through the choir mikes, and we won't be able to push up the volume on the choir without pushing up the volume on the orchestra as well. The orchestra will still drown out the choir."

Well, the orchestra *did* sit on the first row of the choir, and I had fits Sunday morning trying to keep the instruments from drowning out the choir. Needless to say, I wasn't very successful.

I tell this story to illustrate how our perception of an event or person is influenced by our own personal experiences. To Eva and Mel, Hogan came across as haphazardous and disorganized. Compared to Ken, Hogan was a very methodical person who planned very well. While I agree with everything Mel and Eva said on the topic, they have never worked with Ken Tipton.

That discussion on Hogan's planning (or lack thereof) started me thinking. As a result, I began to make comparisons between Ken and Hogan. I wondered if the two were really all that different, with the exception that Hogan is a lot better looking (Sorry Ken!) and technically competent. They both have the same quick wit and they both like being in charge. I began to think, "Wouldn't it be fun to take a Ken-type character, place him in Stalag 13 and make him a private so everybody outranks him?" Our church does a Living Christmas Tree presentation every year at Christmas. This program is Ken's "claim to fame," so I could have this character in a subplot running around camp trying to put on a Living Christmas Tree.

Ken Tipton has never met a person he didn't pick on; and as I said earlier he's got that Hogan quick wit, so it's hard to get one over on him. There is an unwritten rule stating, "Anytime you have the chance to get Ken, take it!" By now, the thoughts in my mind were starting to congeal into a storyline, and I was curious to see if I could come up with a decent story, so I decided to give fictional writing a shot. As a further incentive, I decided it would be fun to give Ken a copy as a gag gift for Christmas.

In August 2000 the writing process began. At the time, I envisioned this as a short story and I never expected it would exceed 20 pages. I could have it written and polished by Christmas with no sweat. As Christmas approached it became obvious the story was turning into a book and there was no way it would be finished. Instead of a completed story, I pulled an Eva and gave Ken what is now Chapter 1 with an IOU for the rest when it was completed. He received an unpolished draft manuscript for Christmas of 2001.

And that, my friends, is the crazy story of how this book came to be in existence. For the benefit of those of you who don't know Ken Tipton, he does have some redeeming character traits, but you will have to read this book and meet his fictional counterpart to find out what they are. I'm not going to tell you.

LaVerne Cash

CHAPTER 1
The Bait is Set

December 1942
London, England

An Axis biological offensive campaign was one of the most feared threats of the war. The latest report from Germany struck fear into the hearts of more than one allied intelligence officer. It read, "Germans highly advanced in BW.[1] Need expert assistance in Düsseldorf. Hot Potato." Hot potato was code for "urgent — right away."

"Where did this information come from?" questioned Mike Anders, an operative for the US Office of Strategic Services (OSS).

"It came by way of a British SIS[2] operative code named 'Pretzel'. A good man," replied Colonel Alistair Wembley,[3] a short, pudgy, bald British Intelligence officer with a bushy black mustache and an abrasive personality.

"It seems kind of cryptic," mused Anders, not quite sure what to think of the message.

"Pretzel is a trusted operative. We have no reason to dispute his word," responded Wembley.

True enough. When it came to espionage, the British certainly seemed to know what they were doing. All the intelligence Anders had seen from the British had been top notch, which was why this message bothered him.

"If he says the Germans are mounting an all-out offensive in biological warfare, then we must act on the information," Wembley said firmly.

"Wait just a minute! Where does it say the Nazis are mounting an all-out offensive? All it says is that the Germans are highly advanced in biological warfare. That could mean anything from they have found an effective vaccine for typhoid to they have found a way to mass-produce the common cold. It's vague!"

"Pretzel says he needs expert assistance, so we will send in one of our top biologist to assess the German effort and determine a way to destroy it."

"Send a top biologist to do what?" shouted Anders. "Get himself captured or killed! You are jumping the gun on this. Even if this message is on the level we still don't know what kind of 'expert' Pretzel needs. We may send in a biologist when what he really needs is ...is... a pilot!"

"Nonsense," chided Wembley, "This is biological warfare we are talking about, which can only mean that they have perfected some biological means of mass destruction. The only possible help he could need would be someone to bring back the pertinent results and determine how to sabotage the effort. In other words, a biologist."

"Not necessarily," argued Anders. "If there is an advancement, and that's a big if, it could be in the delivery mechanism."

"A delivery mechanism is just a bomb. There's nothing revolutionary about bombs."

"Yes, but a bomb works based on an explosive mechanism, an explosion generates heat, heat kills bugs, and dead bugs are useless! If the Nazis have developed a delivery mechanism that doesn't generate heat, Pretzel could need the assistance of an engineer." Anders could feel his blood pressure rising. Wembley seemed to have that effect on people. As Mike's boyhood friend would have said, his Irish temper was starting to show. Only problem was, Mike wasn't Irish.

"Poppycock. Pretzel needs a biologist, so we send in a biologist," contended Wembley.

Wembley was one of those narrow-minded, by-the-book, desk jockeys whose idea of field work was to go down to the corner pub for tea! *He must have bought (or more likely, talked) his way into his rank because otherwise he doesn't know his head from a hole in the ground,* thought Anders. *Well, I guess every group has one.*

"I agree we should send somebody in," Anders rebutted, "but not a biologist, not yet. This should be a reconnaissance mission. Once we have the facts, then we can send in a biologist if the situation warrants it. Right now this whole thing sounds suspicious. I just got back from Germany and I've seen no evidence that the Nazis are mounting any kind of offensive biological effort. As a matter of fact, Hitler is very much opposed to offensive bio[4] and he's not putting a whole lot of emphasis on defensive bio either."

"And just what makes Hitler such a trustworthy source?" retorted Wembley with a snort.

"He's not, but unless one has a vaccine or a treatment for whatever the biological agent unleashed upon the enemy, causalties among friendly troops are going to be just as high as among enemy troops. Hitler knows this, as does most of his general staff. Even his pro-offensive officers are taking Hitler's anti-offensive proclamations very seriously, which indicates to me that he means business. Besides even if the Nazis were mounting an offensive bio effort, why Düsseldorf? It would make more sense to locate it near Lüneburger Heath. Then they would have access to the Raubkammer Proving Ground. All I'm saying is I think we need to check this out a little before we do something we might regret later," replied Anders.

"But," Wembley added, "Düsseldorf has a prisoner-of-war camp nearby, and prisoners make excellent test subjects for biological experimentation."

"It's against the Geneva Convention to use POWs in human experimentation."

"Where does it say that?"

"Article 2: 'They must at all times be humanely treated and protected…'[5]"

"It doesn't explicitly state 'no experimentation on POWs', therefore that article doesn't mean a thing."

"Experimentation on humans does not constitute humane treatment."

"Humph," snorted Wembley, "Hitler doesn't even treat his own people humanely. He can hardly be expected to treat prisoners humanely."

After much debate, the decision was made to send agent Goldilocks to make contact with Pretzel and assess the situation. "Goldilocks" was the code name for a group established earlier in the year as a processing center for downed flyers or escaped prisoners. This group was based out of a German POW camp located near a small village called Hammelburg (not to be confused with the town of Hammelburg located more centrally in Germany). The camp was close to the city of Düsseldorf in western Germany. Recently, Goldilocks ventures had begun to broaden into the sabotage and intelligence arena, a thought which made what little hair Wembley had bristle.

"Goldilocks."

A thought from another life made Anders grin. Growing up he'd had a friend he used to tease with that name, because unlike Anders, his friend was about as far from being a Goldilocks as you could get. Robert was tall with brown eyes and jet-black hair. In fact, Robert looked more like Papa Bear — which made it even more fun to tease him with the "Goldilocks" name. Of course Robert, always one to have the last word, usually retorted with the nickname "Soot Head." Anders was tall and blond with blue eyes. Both Mike and Robert were handsome in different ways, and they loved to compete for the attention of the neighborhood girls. Funny, he hadn't thought about Robert in years. He wondered what Robert was doing now.

Anders wrenched his mind back to the Düsseldorf problem, but decided it would be a good idea to find out more about this prisoner-of-war camp. What was it, Stalag 13? While Hitler may be anti-bio, Himmler certainly was not. Despite the evidence, Anders had to consider the possibility Himmler might be setting up to perform biological experimentation on humans despite the Geneva Convention. As much as he hated to admit it, Wembley did have a point about POWs making excellent test subjects. He should probably check on this Pretzel character as well. For some reason he had a very strange feeling about all of this.

Western Germany

"Goldilocks, we have reports that the Germans are mounting an all-out offensive in biological warfare. One of our agents, code-named 'Pretzel,' is in your area. He has requested a meeting for 2300 hours tonight at the abandoned farmhouse on the Cologne road two kilometers south of your area. Meet him and relay any information he has on the German biological effort back to us immediately," ordered Mama Bear.

Mama Bear was the code name for the London Headquarters from which Goldilocks received their orders. Colonel Wembley was on duty.

"Orders acknowledged," replied Goldilocks. "What type of effort do the Germans have going and where?"

"We haven't a clue, old bean. Since it is in your area, we were rather hoping you could tell us."

"Sorry, old bean," mimicked Goldilocks. "We have seen no evidence of Nazi activity in biological warfare in our area, nor has any been reported by any of our local contacts."

"Well, our man says it's there," quipped Mama Bear. "You chaps are going to have to be more alert if you expect to make it in the intelligence world. Meet Pretzel, find out what's going on, lend any and all assistance he may require, and report back. Mama Bear, out."

Amateurs thought Wembly as he signed off. It had been a pure mistake giving an assignment this important to a group of rogue flyboys who just happened to get lucky a couple of times. Prison was where they belonged. Too bad the Germans didn't maintain a tighter control over their POW camps. He just hoped they didn't manage to get too many real agents killed while playing their "spy games."

"Will do. Goldilocks, out," responded Colonel Robert Hogan as his radioman, Staff Sergeant James Ivan Kinchloe, broke off the connection.

"More alert! What does he mean 'more alert'?" shouted Peter Newkirk, a skinny British Royal Air Force Corporal, angrily, "Tell me, who was it that got the information on the new Tiger tank[6] for them."

"Yeah, and who stole their silent aircraft engine,[7]" retorted an equally angry French Corporal, Louis LeBeau.

Explosives expert Sergeant Andrew Carter started to add his two cents worth, "And who…"

Hogan was trying to think, but having problems drowning out the noise. "Pipe down!" he ordered, "We have more important things to worry about."

"Biological warfare… that's pretty nasty stuff," said Kinchloe, known to his friends as Kinch. "Do you think any of it is on the level, Colonel?"

"I don't know," mused Hogan. "I hope not, but I intend to find out. Tonight!"

Hogan's thoughts troubled him the rest of the day. Conventional warfare was bad enough, but biological warfare was worse, much worse. Each person infected by a bacterium or virus carried by a biological weapon continued to infect others long after the delivery mechanism had done its work.

Hogan was reminded of an incident from his childhood. His next door neighbor and friend, Timothy Sonntag, was one of a brood of thirteen children. One day one of the younger kids came down with the chicken pox. Consequently, Timothy's father refused to let any of the kids go to school or let anyone come over to see them. Hogan and Timothy had to cancel horse back riding plans and Timothy wasn't even sick! Hogan thought the old man had flipped until a few days later when the disease spread like wildfire through the rest of the family. Suddenly Timothy's father was the smartest man in the world. Thanks to Timothy's dad, Hogan and half the town managed to escape the chicken pox. The memory made Hogan shudder. The thoughts of some deadly disease like typhoid, cholera, or the plague running rampant over a population like the chicken pox had over his friend's family sent cold chills down Hogan's back. He had to find out what the Germans had going and stop it!

* * *

"You want to do WHAT?!?!" Hogan shouted at the private standing before him in his office. Hogan was still disturbed by his earlier conversation with London. This wasn't helping any.

Undaunted by the glare of his commanding officer or rise of tone in his voice, Private Ken Tiptoe replied "I want to do something a little out of the ordinary for Christmas this year. I want to put on a program I call a Living Christmas Tree."

"And just what, may I ask, is a 'Living Christmas Tree'?" retorted Hogan, arms folded across his chest, glaring at the private as though he had grown a second head.

"Well, sir," Tiptoe began "A Living Christmas Tree is where a choir presents a program while standing on tiered risers built so that as you go up each riser gets shorter in length until the last riser is a point. When you get all the people on it, it looks like a tree."

Hogan struggled to visualize the concept. "And where are you going to put this thing?"

"Tree, sir," Tiptoe corrected.

"Tree," Hogan continued, "Where are you going to put this *tree?* Where are you going to get the risers? And just how are you going to make this thing look like a tree?"

"We will put it in the rec. hall, sir, and as for the rest, we'll wing it. We'll work it out as we go along. Don't worry, sir, it'll come together. You'll see."

In exasperation Hogan shouted, "May I remind you private, that this is a prison camp? It's not Carnegie Hall. There are only two weeks until Christmas! How do you expect to pull off something like this in two weeks?" This type of behavior was typical of Tiptoe. He always waited for things to fall into place at the last minute. Hogan would have almost bet somebody had to push him out of his burning airplane before it was too late.

"Well, as you know, sir," Tiptoe began, "Some of the other prisoners and I have put together a camp choir and we have been working on some Christmas songs. Johnson's great with design and he can build the risers. Petersen is wonderful with costumes and, of course, I'm a fantastic director." At this Hogan rolled his eyes. "The camp is full of creative people," Tiptoe went on enthusiastically. "We can make it work. I know we can. Besides, Christmas is such a hard time for prisoners what with the war, not getting to be with their families and not knowing when they will ever get to go home again. In some cases, not knowing if there will be a home to go to. It's a tough time. Something special might help brighten Christmas for a lot of the guys."

Tiptoe had found Hogan's soft spot. Hogan sighed. "Ok, I'll ask Klink to let you do a show."

"It's a performance, sir, not a show."

"Whatever," replied Hogan as he let out a breath. "I'll get Klink to let you put on your... your... *performance*."

"Thank you, sir. Thank you very much!" exclaimed a gleeful Tiptoe. "You won't regret this."

Tiptoe nearly bounced out of Hogan's office. Hogan was sure he was going to hit his head on the rafters on the way out. Tiptoe was known around camp as "The Right Irreverent Reverend Ken Tiptoe" among those who could pronounce the word "right" as Tiptoe did with his native Tennessee drawl. To the rest, he was the "minister of harassment." Tiptoe had received his draft notice on the day of his graduation from seminary, exchanging a minister of music position for a bomber's position.

In the three months Tiptoe had been in camp, he had more than earned his nickname. Tiptoe had an acid tongue and a quick wit, which he never hesitated to use on anyone in camp regardless of race, creed, religion, national origin, or rank. The tongue of Tiptoe struck everywhere and everybody. No one, but no one, was exempt. Tiptoe's teasing was never meant to be belligerent and rarely did anybody take offense.

In Hogan's opinion, the person responsible for putting Tiptoe in an airplane should have been shot for treason. Planes and flying were Hogan's passion in life, and Tiptoe was the biggest imbecile he had ever seen at anything the least bit technical. Putting a technical incompetent like Tiptoe anywhere near a plane was criminal! Tiptoe was the only person Hogan had ever seen who could burn out a light bulb just by turning on a switch. Even the usually mild-mannered Kinchloe refused to let Tiptoe within 100 yards of the radio room.

Despite his technical incompetence, Tiptoe had one redeeming trait: he had a real gift for counseling people. As senior officer, Hogan was responsible for the welfare of the men in camp. While he had no problems making sure the men were treated humanely, he had never been comfortable dealing with personal issues, not even his own. With Tiptoe around, he didn't have to. Since the camp had no official chaplain, Tiptoe had taken on the role unofficially. If a prisoner had a problem, it wasn't unusual to find him at Tiptoe's door. Tiptoe had a way of saying just the right thing to make a person feel better. Oddly enough sometimes it was actually the manner in which he picked on the person that did the trick. That one boggled Hogan's mind. Tiptoe's heart was just as big as his mouth. If a prisoner was sick it was usually a race as to who would get to his side first, LeBeau with his chicken soup or Tiptoe with his prayers. Usually Tiptoe won simply because one doesn't have to cook prayers. Hogan had to admit, Tiptoe's willingness to take on the task of helping the men deal with their personal issues had made his life a lot easier.

Later that day Hogan approached the camp kommandant, Wilhem Klink with Tiptoe's idea.

"Colonel Hogan, I have a lot of things to do before I leave tomorrow, so state your business and get out," muttered Klink without looking up.

Hogan acted surprised.

"Oh, you are going somewhere? Not for long I hope. The old stalag just isn't the same without you."

"You know as well as I do, I'll be gone a week."

Then Klink looked up and shook his finger at Hogan as he warned, "And no funny business out of you while I'm gone!"

Hogan feigned hurt as he said, "Kommandant, I'm shocked you would even think a thing like that!"

"Yeah, yeah," replied Klink going back to his work. "What do you want?"

"The men would like permission to put on a 'Live Christmas Tree'," said Hogan matter-of-factly.

"What!?"

Klink jumped up from his chair so fast Hogan thought he was going to make himself dizzy. On the other hand, how could a dizzy person get dizzy? Maybe he would just make himself normal. Now that was a scary thought.

In his best snake oil salesman voice, Hogan replied.

"Some of the men would like to put on a show for Christmas."

A pause, then Hogan rolled his eyes to look at Klink and with that sweet and innocent look that usually meant he was up to something, and said slowly.

"A Live Christmas Tree."

"And just what, Colonel Hogan, is a 'Live Christmas Tree'?" ask Klink in a sarcastic tone meant to put Hogan in his place which, of course, Hogan ignored.

"Well, it's where we go out, find the biggest tree we can find and plant it in the middle of the compound. The chorus climbs the tree and sings Christmas carols while standing on limbs in the tree dressed like ornaments," replied Hogan in a singsong tone of voice that could usually lull Klink into anything he wanted.

"Hogan, that is utterly ridiculous!" replied Klink. "I'm busy. Dismissed."

Hogan hastily added, "Ok, — how about we dress Schultz in green, decorate him, and let LeBeau stand on his shoulders dressed like an angel."

Exasperated Klink yelled, "Colonel Hogan, stop wasting my time! If your chorus wants to do a show they can do it in the rec. hall. Now out! OUT! Before I have you thrown in the cooler!"

"Yes, sir." replied Hogan adopting a more serious demure as he simultaneously saluted and made a hasty exit.

Hogan grinned as he left Klink's office. Since being captured there was nothing Hogan enjoyed more than annoying Klink. Hogan had barely made it out the door into the compound when he was met by Tiptoe.

"So, Colonel. What happened? How did it go?"

"Fine. You can have your show," replied Hogan.

"Performance," corrected Tiptoe.

"Performance," Hogan repeated absent-mindedly, not interested in arguing semantics, his mind refocusing on the horrors of biological warfare.

"Good, by the way I'm going to have an orchestra. Would

you like to play the drums from the top of the tree?" asked Tiptoe with a grin and made his own hasty exit as Hogan gave him a look that told Tiptoe if he said one more word he was in for a court martial.

First London, now Tiptoe. The day was deteriorating rapidly. What else could happen?

Cologne, Germany

"Colonel," addressed the black-clad captain "We just received word. The meeting has been set for 2300 hours tonight at the abandoned farm north of here. The contact's code name is 'Goldilocks'."

"Good," replied Colonel Emil Gottfried. "Have two squads of men assembled and ready to move out at 2200. You will take one squad and approach from the north side. I will take the other and approach from the south. Hide in the woods out of sight until I give the word, then move in quickly, surround, and take him before he has a chance to get away."

"Jawohl, mein colonel," responded the captain as he saluted then turned on his heels and marched away.

Gottfried smiled. Soon the key to all the secrets of the allied biological program would be in his hand. And Gottfried knew how to use a key!

CHAPTER 2
The Trap is Sprung

London, England

*I*nteresting, thought Anders, *British born, British mother, German father. You can't hang a man for having Germany ancestry.* Which was a good thing for him. While Anders himself was as American as they came, both of his parents had immigrated to the US from Germany and eventually settled down in Cleveland, Ohio. He wondered how they were. What had happened to all his siblings? As Robert would say, there was enough of them for a baseball team and then some. Well, Robert was just jealous because he was an only child. Why was he thinking so much about the past lately?

Enough of that! Anders refocused his thoughts on the subject at hand "Pretzel." Pretzel's father had been a taxidermist, his mother a nurse, so it was no surprise that the boy would have an interest in anatomy. Growing up he had worked in his father's shop while attending medical school. After many debates with his professors concerning his techniques, which they found to be controlling and cruel, he dropped out. Because of his German and medical background, the British Special Intelligence Service had recruited Pretzel in 1931 to infiltrate the Nazi party as a member of the newly formed SchutzStaffel,[8] otherwise known as the SS. His job — monitor and report on the German biological efforts. Initially his record for intelligence work was unsurpassed. But as the Nazi party grew in power, Pretzel's intelligence became less reliable. No major screw-ups, but little things like requests for information that "accidentally" found their way into the hands of the Nazis or milk run missions that were only partially successful. As time passed, the mistakes grew worse. Contacts, many top experienced agents, fell into Nazi hands or disappeared entirely, coinciding with assignments involving Pretzel. Most suspiciously, Pretzel had risen through the ranks in the SS much too fast. Had Pretzel turned into a double agent? Was Pretzel luring Goldilocks into a trap? These were disturbing questions. Ones to which Anders had only suspicions but no proof.

Germany

Hogan's men gathered around awaiting final instructions before Hogan's departure to meet Pretzel. He had swapped his uniform for black pants, sweater, and windbreaker. The exposed parts of his body were slathered with black face paint to prevent his being seen in the darkness.

"Are you sure you don't want one of us to go with you?" asked Kinch. For some reason he had felt uneasy about the mission since the call from London.

"I'm a big boy now, I can take care of myself," chided Hogan. "Besides, somebody has to hold down the fort while I'm gone."

"When do you expect to be back, sir?" inquired Newkirk.

"I don't know," admitted Hogan. "It all depends on what information Pretzel has and what he needs."

"Do you think you will be back by roll call?" asked Carter.

"I don't see why not."

LeBeau asked, "What if you aren't? You will be the first person Klink will look for and if you aren't here, boy is he ever going to notice."

"Stick Olsen in one of my uniforms and put him in formation."

"Can't," answered Newkirk, " He's got the measles, I believe they're German. He's in the infirmary."

"Well, then stick Tiptoe in one of them. He's about my size," retorted Hogan. "I'm sure the guys in Barracks 12 can arrange a diversion so that he's not missed. The Krauts are looking for the right number of men. Nobody is going to pay too much attention to one particular private, besides, I'm sure he'd love to be a colonel."

"Yeah, he's pushy enough to be an officer," muttered Newkirk. "Not to imply that you are pushy, sir," Newkirk added hastily as Hogan gave him a hard stare.

Carter chimed in, "Look who is calling whom pushy."

"Pushy, me pushy?!" exclaimed Newkirk "Why I ..."

"Pipe down!" ordered Hogan. "Now promise me you won't destroy the place while I'm gone, fellas."

With a puzzled expression on his face Carter began a reply, "Why would we..."

"Ah, have a nice meeting, sir," interrupted Kinch, saving Carter the embarrassment of showing his ignorance.

Climbing the ladder to the tunnel's entrance, Hogan shouted, "Don't wait up for me."

* * *

Tiptoe was having dreams of Living Christmas Trees and of being the minister of music in his own church. His church was big with a cathedral ceiling perfect for the Living Christmas Tree it hosted each and every Christmas. This tree was built with a steel structure specially designed for the building in which it stood. It stood 37 feet tall with a massive 11-foot light-studded star at the top. It could hold 125 singers, tapering to a point in 10 rows of platforms curved to form a semi-circle in the front of the church. Each row contained two platforms, a loading platform and a performing platform accessed by two ladders, one on each side of the tree. A wall of panels standing about four feet high from each performing platform hid the singing choir. The panels were covered with greenery and decorated with thousands of lights and various ornaments. The entire structure alone, without the performers, actually looked like a giant Christmas tree. The green-robed singers walked out onto the loading platform designed to be out of sight from the audience. They stepped up to the performing platform and crouched behind the panels until a cue was given, then they would pop up, apparently (to the audience) from out of nowhere. Hundreds of people were involved in the production. Thousands more were in attendance each year, all oohing and ahing over the lights, the decorations, the singing, the whole majesty of it all. Of course, they were also in awe of the marvelous director.

Tiptoe awoke with a start. He looked at his watch, it was 2300, or 11:00 p.m. civilian time. Something seemed to be telling him "Pray for the Colonel." He didn't understand it, but if God could talk to a little boy in a temple[9] he could certainly talk to a prisoner in a POW camp. Tiptoe didn't know exactly what he was praying for, but he prayed.

* * *

Hogan paced aimlessly about the barn. He looked at his watch, 2305. A man in his early to mid thirties entered. A little shorter than Hogan, he was wiry with light brown hair and hazel eyes — a rather ordinary looking man.

"Humpty Dumpty sat on a wall," the man said.

"Humpty Dumpty had a great fall," replied Hogan.

"All the kings horses and all the kings men..."

"Ought to be able to write a better code than this!" complained Hogan.

"That's not in the code."

"I can't help it, I hate these hokey codes. I applied for the code-writing department, but I was turned down. Too much creativity."

The man laughed. "I take it you are Goldilocks."

Hogan replied. "Pretzel?"

"Yes," Pretzel responded.

"London tells me you have information on a Nazi biological effort."

"Yes, the Nazi biologists have figured out..." before Pretzel could finish his remark every entrance to the place was bashed open. In a matter of seconds, the old abandoned barn turned into a sea of black uniformed SS men.

A mincing looking officer walked over to Hogan as two other SS men placed them in handcuffs. *A bit of overkill,* thought Hogan. After all, where were they going to go, especially with all these guards. The officer began looking them over.

"You are under arrest for spying!" he announced with a gleam in his eye.

Well, thought Hogan, *at least he isn't Hochsetter.* Thank God for small favors. But how long would it be before Major Hochsetter, the head of the Düsseldorf Gestapo found out? Hochsetter was a frequent visitor to Stalag 13. He would recognize Hogan and then there would be no way out. If he were lucky he would only get shot. If not… no, he wasn't going to think about "if not's." He would play for a break.

As they were herded into a truck, Hogan assumed they would be taken to Gestapo headquarters in Düsseldorf. But Hogan's assumption was wrong. When they reached the fork in the road that led to Düsseldorf, the driver instead took the fork leading to Cologne. Why would an officer from Cologne be in Düsseldorf? Why not turn the matter over to the Düsseldorf Gestapo? At least this way his chances of running into Hochsetter were less. And as the saying goes, he wasn't about to look a gift horse in the mouth.

Sometime later they were lead into an office. The arresting officer smiled as he introduced himself, "I am Colonel Emil Gottfried. We are going to have a little talk. You can begin by telling me who you are."

* * *

As he usually did when someone was out of camp, Kinch slept in the radio room that night. He did so mainly to receive the message if the absent person ran into a problem and needed to call in. Second, his bunk was right over the tunnel entrance. When a person came in from a late night contact, getting back in the barracks meant Kinch had to get up so the passageway could be opened. By sleeping in the radio room, he could actually get some sleep without being disturbed by the inbound operative.

Last night Kinch had not done much sleeping. Partially, it was the idea of the Nazis spreading disease all over the world, but mainly it was the colonel being out alone. He always worried when somebody was out of camp, but the colonel was the life source of the whole operation. He was the one with the ideas, the infectious enthusiasm, the one who could twist the Krauts in so many directions they didn't know which end was up. He was the one leading the way. If anything happened to the colonel, Kinch hated to think about where the rest of them would end up. Yes, Kinch *was* worried about Colonel Hogan. It was 0700. Where was he?

"Hey, sleepy head! Get up! It will be time for roll call in a couple of hours and LeBeau's making a 'special breakfast'. We are evaluating the camp," ribbed Newkirk as he stepped over the bunk frame onto the ladder and jumped to the floor. "What time did the colonel get back? I was having this marvelous dream about being stranded on a deserted island with this gorgeous redhead and didn't hear him come in."

"That's because he didn't come in," replied Kinch worriedly. "He should have been back hours ago."

"Maybe he found my redhead and went out on a date," retorted Newkirk. "I mean, you know the colonel and girls and time does fly when you are having fun."

Walking over to the radio, Kinch retorted, "That's not funny!"

"Sorry, just trying to lighten things up a bit. Maybe the mission got involved and he was delayed," responded Newkirk, becoming more serious after Kinch's rebuff. *The colonel was all right. He had to be!*

Kinch replied, "If that were the case, he would have contacted us. I've got a feeling he's in some kind of trouble."

"You know the governor, he has a golden tongue. He can talk his way out of anything. There's still a couple of hours `til roll call, he'll be back," said Newkirk cheerfully.

"Do you really believe that?" asked Kinch softly sitting down at the radio.

I want to believe it. Newkirk looked downcast. "I was hoping you'd believe it and convince me," he muttered.

The sounds of Kinch tapping out code distracted Newkirk from his thoughts.

"Hey, what are you are doing?"

"I'm sending a message to the underground units to see if they know anything."

"Good idea. I'll go tell the others," replied Newkirk as he scampered up the ladder back into the common room.

LeBeau was having a grand time cooking while the other occupants of Barracks 2 were in varying states of readiness, preparing to start the day.

"Smells good. What is it?" asked Carter.

"Quiche Lorraine," responded LeBeau with pride.

"I knew a girl named Lorraine once back home," Carter injected. Suddenly in alarm, he shouted, "Hey! You didn't put Lorraine in there did you?"

"No I didn't put Lorraine or anybody else in there. What do you think I am, a cannibal?" retorted LeBeau angrily.

As Newkirk returned to the room LeBeau commented, "Colonel Hogan must have been out awfully late last night. I haven't heard a sound from his room and he is usually up by now. Maybe somebody should wake him."

"Forget it mate!" said Newkirk, "You haven't heard him because he's not there. He didn't come back last night."

"What!?" shouted LeBeau and Carter simultaneously.

"You heard me. He didn't come back." Newkirk replied defensively.

"Where is he? What happened?" LeBeau was dazed by the news. *Please let the colonel be all right, please!*

"I don't know," admitted Newkirk. "Kinch is on the radio now trying to get some answers. In the meantime we better come up with a cover for him at roll call. A couple of candy bars will take care of Schultz, but Klink won't be so easy."

"Yeah," Carter responded. "With him going away on leave, he's going to want Colonel Hogan's advice on girls."

"Well, with Klink that would take more than advice, it would take a ruddy miracle," proclaimed Newkirk dourly. His expression suddenly brightened as he exclaimed, "I've got an idea!"

"Where are you going?" asked Carter as Newkirk rushed for the door.

"To Barracks 12. To get Tiptoe," answered Newkirk.

"Tiptoe's not going to fool Klink," said LeBeau.

"No, but he'll do for roll call. I've got another idea for handling Klink," responded Newkirk, closing the door behind him.

* * *

Tiptoe had just finished shaving and was admiring himself in the mirror when Newkirk came in. *Best looking man in camp,* he thought. What few women came through camp thought Hogan was, but they were blinded by his eagles. If Tiptoe had eagles... well, it was a good thing for the women of the world that he didn't.

"Come on, private, let's go," ordered Newkirk.

"Where are we going? It's almost time for roll call," responded Tiptoe.

"Don't the Yanks teach you guys anything at all about obeying orders? Don't ask questions. Let's go!" retorted Newkirk.

"Yes, sir."

Tiptoe hated the Army. He hated the fact that everybody had to look alike, act alike — the whole cookie-cutter format — and worst of all, he hated taking orders. The problem with being a private was he was the end of the line. A private was expected to obey orders from anybody and everybody with no one to pass orders down to, and Tiptoe was a man who liked to be in charge.

Newkirk led Tiptoe into Hogan's office followed by LeBeau and Carter.

"Whatever it is, I didn't do it!" began Tiptoe defensively, "And if I did do it, I promise I won't do it again."

"No," began Newkirk handing Tiptoe Hogan's uniform, "but you are going to do it. Congratulations, private, you are now a colonel!"

"What is this? I don't understand. What's going on?" asked Tiptoe, confusion in his voice. "I could get court martialed for impersonating an officer."

"We can all get shot if you don't. Colonel Hogan went out to meet an agent last night and hasn't come back. We need you to cover for him at roll call. All you have to do is put on the colonel's uniform and stand in his place in formation. We will do the rest," explained LeBeau.

"Where is Colonel Hogan? Is he ok? What happened?"

Tiptoe's mind was racing. This didn't sound good. The fact that he was being drafted as a last minute fill-in suggested something had gone awry. Tiptoe was suddenly haunted by the strange urge he had in the night to pray for the colonel. Was it related to the events happening now?

"We don't know," admitted Newkirk. "We expected him back before now. Kinch is on the radio now trying to find out. In the meantime, we all have to pull together and cover for him until he gets back. Fortunately, Klink is going on leave this morning and will be gone for a week. His temporary replacement is new to camp, so he won't know that you aren't the colonel. That will buy us time to find out what's going on."

"What about Schultz? He'll know I'm not Hogan."

"Schultz isn't a problem. We can handle him," piped in Carter.

Newkirk added, "We will see to it that Klink doesn't get close enough to you to realize you aren't Hogan, but you are going to have to do one thing. No matter what happens you are going to have to keep your mouth shut. Don't say a word."

"Why? I can hold my own in a battle of wits," retorted Tiptoe defensively.

"Yes, but the colonel doesn't speak like a ... How do you Americans say 'hill berry'?" replied LeBeau.

Carter corrected him, " 'Hillbilly', the word is 'hillbilly'. And he also wears shoes."

"I wear shoes!" responded Tiptoe angrily. "What's with the stereotyping? Just because I'm from Tennessee and I talk a little differently, does that make me a moron? I..." then he looked down at his feet. They were bare. He had been changing into Hogan's uniform while they were talking and had not put on the shoes. Well, he *was* from the hills of Tennessee. Maybe he really was a hillbilly. He laughed! They all laughed. Tiptoe noted, *Point to remember, don't jump to conclusions.*

* * *

"ROLL CALL! ROLL CALL! Everybody out for roll call!" shouted Sergeant Hans Schultz as he entered Barracks 2.

"Ok, Schultz, you don't have to yell, we can hear. We can hear!" said LeBeau filing out the door.

"Yeah, we aren't deaf!" Carter added.

Outside, all the prisoners lined up in their usual spots with Tiptoe in Hogan's. Kinch's spot was empty. As Schultz went down his roster, Kinch slipped quietly into place moments before his name was read.

"Anything?" inquired Newkirk.

"Not a thing," responded Kinch.

Schultz walked down the line. Tiptoe, in Hogan's place, had adopted the colonel's cocky, self-confident stance. In Hogan's uniform, unless one looked closely, it would be hard to tell it wasn't Hogan standing there. Both men were about the same height and had the same dark hair coloring. Tiptoe was a bit smaller than Hogan, but aside from that they were built roughly the same. Schultz passed Tiptoe without a look, then he backed up and looked again.

"You are not Colonel Hogan!" shouted Schultz at Tiptoe as Tiptoe silently feigned shock.

"He's not Colonel Hogan? Are you sure, Schultzy?" queried Newkirk.

"He is not Colonel Hogan! Where is Colonel Hogan?" shouted Schultz again.

"Well, what does Colonel Hogan look like?" asked LeBeau innocently.

"You know what Colonel Hogan looks like," exclaimed an exasperated Schultz. "He's about this high," indicating Hogan's height with his hand. "He has black hair and brown eyes."

Carter looked at Tiptoe then back at Schultz and repeated, "This high, black hair, brown eyes? Yep, that's Colonel Hogan."

"He is not Colonel Hogan! The Kommandant will be here any minute, now where is Colonel Hogan?" shouted Schultz getting frantic.

"He's right here, in formation where he's supposed to be," replied Newkirk taking a candy bar out of his pocket.

Schultz looked Tiptoe over from head to toe.

"He does look like Colonel Hogan."

"He *is* Colonel Hogan!" responded LeBeau as Newkirk took another candy bar out of his pocket.

"But why isn't he talking? Colonel Hogan is never this quiet," Schultz observed.

"Because he's got laryngitis," added Kinch.

Apparently baffled, Schultz repeated the word slowly, "Lar-yn-gi-tis?"

"Yeah, It means he can't talk," explained Carter as Tiptoe moved his lips and made gestures. Newkirk pulled out yet another candy bar.

"Too bad, Colonel Hogan. I hope you get to feeling better," said Schultz as he took the candy bars and went about his business.

"All present and accounted for," reported Schultz as Klink came out of his office with another officer in tow.

"Gentlemen," addressed Klink, "This is Major Roth. He will be taking over Stalag 13 temporarily while I am away. Don't get any ideas about escaping because Major Roth will be running this camp with the same iron efficiency that I do. Dismissed!" shouted Klink and returned to his office.

Tiptoe strolled causally into Barracks 2, hurriedly took off Hogan's jacket and put on his own, pulling it up carefully around the collar to hide the eagles on Hogan's uniform. He then scampered down the tunnel and across to his own barracks and emerged just in time to be accounted for there. Tiptoe would return to Hogan's barracks and change back into his own uniform later.

* * *

Gottfried questioned Hogan and Pretzel all through the night. Hogan continuously glazed impassively at the officer with that smug, arrogant, self-confident look that always drove Klink crazy. As the son of an alcoholic ex-cop, he had learned early in life the best way to deal with his father's drunken ranting was to not react to them at all. It was a lesson he had learned very well and had served him equally well during his time in captivity.

There were some things that just weren't making sense. First of all, with the exception of some cursory questions, Gottfried had addressed his inquiries and later his threats almost solely to Hogan. Why? Why not both of them? Then there was Pretzel. Hogan thought that the average spy had nerves of steels and was trained not to flinch at anything, yet the man looked ready to fall apart when Gottfried commenced raving at them. Why?

Hogan was pondering these questions later as he and Pretzel were taken to their cell.

"So, what do you think they are going to do?" questioned Pretzel fearfully.

"Leave us in here for a while to sweat and ponder our fates, then scream and yell some more. Beyond that I haven't a clue," answered Hogan. Truth was he really didn't want to think about it.

"Do you have any ideas for getting out of here?"

"Nope," responded Hogan. "Not a one."

Why had they put the two of them together in the same cell? Overpopulation didn't appear to be a problem, not that Hogan could tell. It made no sense psychologically. Two minds collectively were much more effective than two minds separately. In separate cells all they could do would be to contemplate their fates which, as Gottfried painted, weren't too pleasant. That alone might make either of then more susceptible to talking. Together, at the very least, they could distract each other from such morbid thoughts.

"The Nazis have figured out how to mass-produce plague. Himmler himself ordered the establishment of the Institute for Entomology of the Waffen-SS and Police just for that purpose.[10] They are planning to bring it into Düsseldorf where it will be shipped to London for their agents to release. If that happens, without an antidote the results could be catastrophic," said Pretzel.

"Sounds like something those Nazi monsters would do," responded Hogan.

And that was another thing that bothered Hogan. The man was too talkative for a spy. Hogan caught the brief look of pure unadulterated anger that crossed Pretzel's face at the phrase 'Nazi monsters', Suddenly everything made sense. *Of course, this whole thing is a setup! So that's why they put the two of us together. Bug the cell, prime the pump, and get information from our conversation. Well, two can play that little game.*

"We can only hope that the RAF can drop those potato beetle and cattle plague loads first."

Pretzel agreed, "Yes. Let's hope so. Weren't they supposed to have arrived in England last week? I would have thought they would have them in the air by now. What is the hold up?"

"I... I don't want to talk about it," replied Hogan sheepishly. "I've said too much already. Right now the less you know, the better."

As Hogan expected, once Gottfried realized he wasn't going to talk, it wasn't long before the guard came for Pretzel. Well, now at least he could think. He didn't know how much of what Pretzel had told him was true, but he did know he had to think of a way out.

Monsters, how dare he! thought Ernst Lang, known to Hogan as Pretzel. *The British and the French get away with that barbaric Versailles Treaty following World War I and nobody considers them to be monsters. That ghastly treaty made insane reparation demands[11] of*

Germany, then striped the country of all territories that would provide the means to make payments, thereby nearly destroying the German economy and the German people. Innocent people — women, children, and the elderly who had nothing to do with the war suffered while the high and mighty Americans sat across the ocean doing nothing.[12] When the German government responds in the only way it can to preserve its people, the rest of the world considers it to be a monster.

Lang walked into Gottfried's office. "I assume you heard," stated Lang with disgust. "The Allies are attacking our food sources. Those beasts! At least now we know and can begin defensive strategies."

"Yes," began Gottfried contemplatively "If he is telling the truth, it is a start. In which case, I want to know how the potato beetles were bred and if the allies have developed a defense for them. If so, I want to know what that defense is. I also want to know what biological toxins the Allies are working on, if they have vaccines for them and what those vaccines are. I want to know everything he knows!"

Lang responded, "I can find out. I will go back in, talk to him and get him to tell me. He thinks I'm on his side. He has no reason not to trust to me."

"That will not work. This one is not the chatty type. He's too suspicious. He trusts no one. Besides, there are other ways," replied Gottifried. *Much more pleasurable ways* thought Gottfried with a grin as he considered the means he might use.

* * *

"Hey, fellas! Klink's coming!" yelled Carter from the door.

All the men of Barracks 2 made a mad dash for casual-looking positions. Carter sat on his bunk carving a stick while Newkirk and LeBeau started a card game. Klink pounced in unceremoniously and walked straight to Hogan's quarters. He knocked on the door, walked in, and immediately walked out. "Where is Colonel Hogan?" he bellowed.

Newkirk responded without batting an eyelash, "The colonel went over to Barracks 9, I believe. Bit of trouble over there. Seems some of the guys were having a problem with their Red Cross packages."

"What problem with the Red Cross packages?" Klink asked quizzically.

"Oh, a couple of them were accusing each other of stealing from the packages," responded Carter innocently.

In Barracks 9 Klink's inquiry was met with "Hey, anybody, seen Colonel Hogan?" from Sergeant David Marshall.

The question generated a chorus of "No. No, not me. Haven't seen him all day."

"No, the Colonel's not here," answered Marshall.

"What about that problem he came over to deal with?" asked Klink.

"No problem here, sir, I think that may have been in Barracks 10, but since you brought up problems, the food lately has been really lousy. Can we have cheeseburgers for dinner tonight?"

"NO!" shouted Klink, proceeding to stomp off toward Barracks 10.

Barracks 10 was an instant replay of the Barracks 9 scene except this time he was sent to Barracks 12. In Barracks 12 a response of "Colonel who?" was added to the chorus after which Klink was sent to the mess hall. From the mess hall Klink was sent to the motor pool. The motor pool sent him to the rec. hall where Private Tiptoe was holding a rehearsal, otherwise known as "Tree Practice", for the Living Christmas Tree.

Tiptoe greeted Klink. "Welcome, Kommantant! Have you come to sing with us? I think that is a lovely gesture, the prison kommantant singing with the men. It will mean a lot to them, sir. Now what do you sing: first tenor, second tenor, baritone, bass?"

"I'm not here to sing, private!" shouted Klink. "I'm here to see Colonel Hogan."

"Who?" inquired Tiptoe innocently.

"You know who I'm talking about! Colonel Hogan!" blustered Klink at his wits' end.

"Oh, you mean that American guy with eagles on his shoulders that looks a lot like me, except not as good looking?" quizzed Tiptoe with a smirk on his face.

Exasperated Klink responded, "Yes, that's the one, where is he?"

"He's not here, but will I do?"

"Yes, you will do quite well," said Klink sarcastically. "In the cooler!"

"I'd like to help you out, sir, but I'm afraid I can't," interjected Tiptoe smugly. "I have to direct!"

Klink shook his fist, whirled on his heels, and walked away. The insolence of that man! He was worse than Hogan—if that were possible. It was bad enough having Hogan in the camp. Now there were two of them! Well, Tiptoe at least was Hogan's problem. Hogan deserved it! In the meantime Klink had forgotten what he wanted to talk to Hogan about anyway. A week away from Hogan would do him good. Maybe if he were lucky Hogan would escape while he was gone and take Tiptoe with him. He would almost be willing to spoil his perfect no escape record for such an event.

"OK, guys thanks for coming today," began Tiptoe as he looked out across a sea of crestfallen faces.

In the short time Tiptoe had been at Stalag 13, he had never seen the overall morale so low. Out of necessity the whole camp knew about Hogan's disappearance and it had them on edge. Right after roll call Newkirk, LeBeau and Carter had gone from barracks to barracks explaining the situation and enlisting the aid of their fellow inmates in sending Klink on a wild goose chase designed to keep him from discovering Hogan's absence.

Even though Hogan's actual group of saboteurs was small, he had managed to rally the entire camp round his cause and make it theirs. By making them feel they were a part of something vitally important, something bigger than they, Hogan had taken away that feeling of helplessness each of them had upon capture and restored a sense of dignity and self worth. Hogan took his responsibility to his men very seriously. He could con Klink into just about anything he wanted and took great delight in doing so, yet his requests were always to benefit the men and never himself, things like extra electricity and extra rations.

"Mark, go watch the door a minute, will ya?"

Private Mark Singer ran over to the door of the rec. hall, opened it slightly, and peaked out.

"All clear," Singer announced and continued watching.

"By now I suppose everybody has heard that Colonel Hogan went out on a mission last night and hasn't come back. Well, I just want you to know, I've been promoted to colonel, so everything is going to be just fine."

Tiptoe's comment invoked some grins and a few snickers.

"Seriously, most of you are probably scared. I know I am. It's nothing to be ashamed of. A lot of you are worried about what's going to happen. Some of you are worried about the colonel.

"I know all of us here have different religious beliefs and some don't believe in God at all, but I believe God loves us and God is in control. It may not seem like it at times, it may not seem like it now, but He's here. When things happen it's for a reason. We may not understand God's reasons, but one thing is for sure, He will never put more on us than with His help we can bear. So let's take a few moments to pray."

Every head was bowed and the quiet mutterings of prayers in a variety of languages could be heard as Tiptoe prayed aloud.

"Father we thank you that you are a God of love and a God of mercy. Lord, we ask that you put your hand upon the men in this camp in this time of turmoil. We ask for your guidance, your peace, and your strength. We especially ask that you be with Colonel Hogan. We ask your comfort be upon him wherever he is. We also ask you to give him strength for whatever it is he must face. Lord, we also ask for your guidance upon those trying to determine his fate, those trying to fill his shoes in his absence, and those just waiting. Sometimes waiting is the hardest thing to do, yet sometimes it is what you ask of us. In Jesus' name, amen. Now let's sing!"

* * *

The radio room was a hot bed of activity, as various underground units began reporting back results of their investigations. Kinch was taking advantage of a lull in the activity to stretch his legs when his friend Sergeant Richard Baker walked in.

"You look beat," observed Baker. "I'll take over for a while if you would like to take a break." Baker, like Kinch, had been a radio operator prior to his capture.

"That's ok, staying busy keeps my mind off thoughts I'd rather not be thinking right now, but thanks for the offer," responded Kinch.

"Yeah, I know what you mean. Any news?" questioned Baker.

"Not, yet," sighed Kinch. "You know, it doesn't make sense. Hochsetter knows Colonel Hogan. If the Gestapo has him, Hochsetter should have found out by now and been all over this camp, but instead nobody knows anything. It's as though the colonel dropped off the face of the earth. Or as Carter said 'He was kidnapped by aliens from another planet'."

Baker snickered, "Carter has quite an imagination." There was a moment of hesitation before Baker began again, "I hate to even bring this up, but do you think he might be… ah…"

"Dead?" finished Kinch. "Yeah, I've thought of that. But if he were, then somewhere there would be a body and somebody would know something about it. So far there is absolutely nothing. This probably sounds horrible, but there is a part of me that hopes he is dead. If he is alive, more than likely the Gestapo has him or else he would have found a way to get in touch with us by now. At least if he's dead, he's not suffering. I don't even like thinking about what the Gestapo may be doing to him if he's alive." *Or for that matter, what they would do to any of us if they find out about our operation.*

"I don't think it sounds horrible at all," admitted Baker. "I think it sounds very humane. I don't know the Colonel well, but from the little I do know, he seems like a decent guy. He deserves better than torture at the hands of the Gestapo. Nobody deserves that."

"Yeah," Kinch responded weakly. "Well, one way or the other, I have to know what happened to him."

"Has London been notified?"

"Not yet," answered Kinch. "I had hoped to have at least some information for them. I mean, how do you tell London High Command that you just lost a full colonel. I mean, it's not like losing a button. Anyway, I'm going to have to tell them something soon."

"If there is anything I can do to help, let me know," offered Baker.

Before Kinch could get out a response, a radio signal began coming in. Kinch and Baker exchanged looks.

"Did you hear what I heard?" Kinch asked.

"If what you heard is that Moonglow has some information, yeah, I heard it," replied Baker.

Kinch requested a repeat of the message and took down the information with Baker double-checking him. One of Moonglow's contacts from south of Düsseldorf had reported some activity of the Cologne Gestapo around 2200. Two squads of SS troopers had been seen moving north of Cologne toward what appeared to be an abandoned farm just south of Düsseldorf. Two heavily guarded prisoners were seen being escorted into Gestapo headquarters in Cologne later that night. One fit Hogan's description. The Cologne underground was working with Moonglow on confirming the identity of the prisoners.

* * *

Hogan sat on the bunk with one leg bent and his arm causally draped over the knee. His bravado meant to hide his fear with arrogance and disrespect as Gottfried strolled into the cell with two of the biggest, burliest guards Hogan had ever seen. Whatever Gottfried did to him, Hogan was determined not to make it easy.

"Why, Colonel," exclaimed Hogan with feigned delight. "What a pleasure to see you again! It's been so long. Please forgive the mess, but I really wasn't expecting company today. If you'll come back this afternoon, I'll bake a cake and we can have tea..."

Hogan's chattering came to an abrupt halt as Gottfried slapped him so hard it nearly jarred loose his fillings. He fell back onto the bunk in a daze. Before he could react, one of the guards jerked him up and forced him onto his knees. When he tried to stand he was pushed back down. Each guard grabbed an arm, pulled it behind his back, and twisted it while pushing on his shoulder blades. Hogan winced in pain.

"That's much better," Gottfried replied, walking over to Hogan and looking down at him. "Now, Herr Goldilocks, I am through playing games with you. You will tell me not only who you are, but you will tell me everything you know about the allied biological efforts and anything else I want to know."

And I'll see you in HELL first!! thought Hogan as he looked Gottfried straight in the eye with steely resolve at the same time wishing he had kept his mouth shut about potato beetles and cattle plague.

Gottfried pulled out a dagger from a sheave attached to his belt. He grabbed Hogan by the hair and pulled, forcing his head back, and placed the dagger to Hogan's throat. Hogan remained silent.

"The Gestapo has ways of making people talk. Very unpleasant ways," touted Gottfried smirking.

What do they do? Send these guys to school for this? thought Hogan. Gestapo interrogation 101, tell the prisoner a hundred thousand times, "The Gestapo has ways of making people talk. Very unpleasant ways." It will drive them insane and in their insanity, they will tell you everything you want to know. Well it wasn't going to work with him. Besides he really didn't know anything, at least, not about biological warfare.

"There are ways of inflicting pain — excruciating, lingering pain," Gottfried began mincingly, emphasizing every word. "Some methods end in a slow torturous death, others cause pain without fatality, and others don't even leave a mark."

Gottfried smiled a hideous smile that sent cold chills down Hogan's spine, although outwardly he remained impassive.

"Resist all you can. In the end it will do you no good. You will tell me everything I want to know. And I..." pressing the knife harder against Hogan's throat, Gottfried smiled insidiously, obviously enjoying himself "... I shall derive a great deal of pleasure from your vain struggles and screams."

Gottfried paused for a second, putting the dagger down. As if on cue, both guards simultaneously began to twist Hogan's arms. Hogan winced once more and managed to stifle a groan. Gottfried looked Hogan over as if seeing him for the first time.

"Pretty boy!" Gottfried exclaimed. His eyes were gleaming with delight, as he scraped some of the face paint off Hogan's cheek with his dagger, taking a layer of skin with it.

"Underneath the dirt it looks like we have a pretty boy here. Let us introduce pretty boy to some of our *pleasures*," said Gottfried with a smile that was pure evil.

As the guards jerked Hogan roughly to his feet, and shoved him toward the door, he nearly collided with the officer entering the cell.

"Colonel, there has been a fire at the fuel depot just outside town. Your presence is requested at once. Do you wish for me to continue the interrogation of the prisoner?"

"NO!" was the impassioned response of the colonel looking at the officer. "I will handle it myself upon my return."

The officer clicked his heels, saluted, and left. Gottfried turned his attention back to Hogan.

"It would appear that you have received a reprieve."

Enjoy it while you can. It will be the last peace you will ever know.

"My men know I tolerate no mistakes. If a prisoner escapes, the one responsible takes his place; therefore, they will be on their guard and alert. You can expect no help from within or without. For you, there is no hope.

"Contemplate the situation. I'm sure you will see reason. In any event, we will resume this matter later. Then..." said Gottfried, the evil smile returning as he tenderly wiped blood from Hogan's cheek.

The touch made Hogan's skin crawl. He instinctively paled in response. If it were possible for a human being to melt, Hogan would have. It took every ounce of strength Hogan possessed, and from some source Hogan couldn't identify, to look Gottfried in the eye and gaze at him with an impassive cold hard stare, but somehow he did.

"And then it will be my turn, pretty boy. One way or the other, I WILL have the information I seek."

And my fun as well. Who knows, you may provide me with pleasure for days.

With that the colonel left the cell. The guards threw Hogan onto the bunk and left as well. As he heard the cell door being locked, Hogan collapsed totally and completely drained — mind, body, and spirit, knowing the worse was yet to come.

CHAPTER 3
Death Pays a Visit

England

A nders and Wembley were having yet another round on the "Pretzel" issue.

"I'm telling you there is something very wrong going on here," exclaimed Anders impatiently.

"Pretzel is a…" began Wembley.

"Most trusted agent," finished Anders exasperated. "Yeah, I know, I know. That may have been true ten years ago, but look at now! What has he given us recently? You at least consider have to the fact he maybe a double agent. If so, we may have sent Goldilocks into a trap. By the way, has Goldilocks reported in yet?"

"No," responded Wembley. "But with that group, it doesn't mean anything."

Anders feared the worst. Goldilocks should have reported in a long time ago. If he were lucky, he was dead, but more likely he was in the hands of the Gestapo.

The ring of the phone interrupted Anders thoughts. "Yes, I'll be right there," he heard Wembley say.

"Communications room reports a call from Goldilocks," announced Wembley. "There goes your theory about Pretzel being a double agent. Hogan probably got wrapped up in one of his bizarre schemes and forgot the rest of us are fighting a war. He really should leave the espionage to people who know what they are doing."

Anders choked down a response and followed Wembley to the communications room.

"Go ahead, Goldilocks."

"Colonel Hogan has been captured by the Gestapo and is currently being held at Gestapo headquarters in Cologne," reported Goldlocks.

I was right! thought Anders. Oh, how he wished he had been wrong. Allied High Command would write Hogan off as a casualty-of-war and that would be that. Depending on the mood they were in, they might send in another officer to command his unit. They might, on a good day, even authorize a mass escape for the men left in Stalag 13, but Hogan himself was a statistic, no human being with feelings who could experience pain. By the time the Gestapo finished with Hogan, he would be an expert on pain. That is, if he lived.

"Are you sure?" inquired Wembley.

"Affirmative," replied Goldilocks. "The report was made by Moonglow. We just received confirmation by Nighthawk 15 minutes ago. Request permission to attempt rescue."

Anders came to a decision.

"Hold up!" he shouted, "I'm going in."

"Stand by, Goldilocks," instructed Wembley.

"Whatever are you talking about? Are you daft, man?"

"Maybe, but I'm going in!" retorted Anders, determination evident in his voice.

"For what? For Hogan? He's a renegade pilot playing 'spy games,' putting seasoned agents at undue risk. Small loss, we are better off without him really," replied Wembly impassively.

"Tell that to his mother!" cried Anders in a rage. "Tell her that her only child was tortured to death in a Gestapo prison and is never coming home. I'm sure she wouldn't consider it a 'small loss'. Tell the families of the 100-plus men of Stalag 13 after Hogan breaks and the Gestapo holds a mass execution. I doubt they would consider it a 'small loss' either."

"It's a fact of war. Death happens," Wembley appeared unmoved. "This is all highly irregular. Not to mention unauthorized."

"Like it or not, authorized or not, I'm going in! I'm going to find out once and for all what's going on and fix it if I can. If Pretzel is a double agent, I'm going to bring him to justice. If not, I will apologize a thousand fold if I find him. *AND* I'm going to try and get Hogan out as well," Anders replied in an authoritative voice allowing no discussion and no dissension.

"As you wish, it's your funeral," Wembley replied in a matter-of-fact tone that infuriated Anders further.

"Goldilocks," said Wembley, resuming his conversation with the unit.

"Yes, we're here," responded Goldilocks.

"We are sending an OSS agent to take command of your unit and assess the situation. He will meet you at 2200, sector A14."

"Roger, Mama Bear. Over and out," responded Goldilocks.

"Satisfied?" Wembley asked Anders

"Satisfied," replied Anders as he made his way to the door. He had a few things to take care of before he left for Germany.

Wembley stopped him, "By the way, how do you know Hogan is an only child?"

Anders grinned as he responded, "I read it in his file."

Germany

"What about the colonel? What did London say about getting the colonel out?" asked Carter.

"They didn't say anything," replied Kinch "Only that they were sending in an OSS agent to take command and 'assess the situation'."

"Translation: London has written the colonel off and they are sending this OSS clown to determine whether or not to write the whole lot of us off as well. Bloody charming," announced Newkirk bitterly.

"I don't know who's worse, the Gestapo or the brass," an angry LeBeau shouted.

"The Gestapo are all animals and everybody knows it. Brass on the other hand are all smiles and reassurances," LeBeau said sweetly, then his voice turned bitter, "Until there is trouble, and then they hang you out to dry!"

"Well," interjected Carter sheepishly, "Maybe this guy will help us get the colonel out."

"Aw, you're dreaming, mate," replied Newkirk skeptically.

"Wait a minute," interjected Kinch. "Carter may be onto something. If London were flat out planning on replacing Colonel Hogan, they would have sent in a military officer. This guy is a civilian, OSS. They're loners, undercover guys, they don't work as part of permanent units."

"You can't be saying you think this guy is coming to help us get Colonel Hogan back, can you?" responded LeBeau.

"No, I'm not saying that, but you can't rule it out either. London may be as confused as we are."

"Situation normal," interjected Newkirk.

Kinch ignored Newkirk and continued, "When I asked for permission for a rescue mission, before I was cut off, I heard someone in the background. I couldn't make out what he was saying, but the impression I got was there was some disagreement over how to handle the situation. Maybe 'assessing the situation' means just that."

"Yeah," piped in Carter enthusiastically, "Colonel Hogan is an officer and he cares about people. Remember a couple of months ago when he broke us out of Stalag 4 after that German patrol picked us up? [13] I mean, he could have left us there, you know. If he cares, maybe other officers do too."

"That's it!" exclaimed Newkirk. "That's how we get him out!"

"What did I say?" asked Carter, confusion written all over his face.

"Remember how the colonel got us out?" asked Newkirk.

"I remember. He dressed Schultz up like Klink and sent him to pick us up." LeBeau snickered, "The Kraut just let us go. Frankly, I never knew Schultz could scream and yell so."

"It wasn't easy getting Schultz to agree to go, much less getting him to act arrogantly," mused Kinch. "We coached him all night. You weren't here, but the whole thing was a nightmare. It was the only time I've ever seen the colonel at his wits' end. I seriously think he aged ten years on that one."

For a moment there was silence as the three men stared at the floor. Finally Newkirk said, "Well, now it's his turn. I say we go get *him!*"

"Hey, didn't the underground say something about the Gestapo picking up another guy with the colonel?" asked Carter timidly. "I bet he was the fella Colonel Hogan was supposed to meet. What about him? We can't just leave him there."

"If we can, we'll get him out too, but our first priority has to be the colonel," answered Newkirk. "If we can get the colonel out, maybe he can think of a way to get the other guy out."

Newkirk's comment invoked a general agreement among all of them.

Kinch raised a question "Fine, but what do we tell London? They didn't actually ok a rescue mission."

"And they didn't exactly say 'no' either, now did they, mate?" came Newkirk's reply. "I say we tell them nothing until we get the colonel back, then let him handle it."

"You are never going to get Schultz to go into Gestapo headquarters and pretend to be Klink," chimed Carter. "He's just never going to do it. Besides the Gestapo would never turn Colonel Hogan over to Klink. Maybe we should wait for this OSS guy."

LeBeau retorted angrily, "And give the filthy Bosch more time to work on the colonel. God only knows what they have done to him now. I say we go get him then send this OSS bean counter packing."

"LeBeau's got a point. Even if we give this OSS guy the benefit of the doubt," that comment drew a snort from Newkirk which Kinchloe ignored, "the quicker we move the less time the Gestapo has to work on the colonel. I don't think Newkirk is suggesting we send Schultz in as Klink, but that one of us goes in as a high ranking SS officer."

"Absolutely correct!" replied Newkirk as he went on to explain, "We go in claiming to be from Berlin headquarters and say we have orders to transfer the prisoner."

"It might just work," said Kinch. "I can draw up some fake papers. We'll need a truck and some volunteers to go as escorts."

"Why?" asked Carter "There are three of us, isn't that enough?"

"Because according to the underground, the Gestapo thinks the colonel is some big shot expert in biological warfare. They would never believe just an officer and two guards for an important prisoner like that. We have to be menacing. We need at least four or five and they have to be big," answered Newkirk.

"Well, what are we waiting for? We've got work to do. Let's get going," shouted LeBeau.

"Right. Kinch, you get started on those papers. Carter, you find us some volunteers. Make sure they're muscle men. I'll handle the truck and LeBeau, you take care of the uniforms," ordered Newkirk as the men all hurried off to their perspective jobs. The sooner they got going, the sooner the colonel would be back and this nightmare would be over.

England

"Abwehr, Major Teppel[14] here," responded the German voice on the other end of the phone.

"How is your Aunt Viktoria doing?" asked Anders in perfect German.

"She is as deaf as ever."

"Hans, this is Mike Anders. I don't know if you remember me, it's been some time."

"Yes, I remember you. How could I forget? As I recall, you had quite a thing for the frauleins," answered Teppel.

"Well, you know how it goes..." responded Anders sheepishly, "All work and no play makes Jack a dull boy."

"I don't think you need worry about being a dull boy even though your name isn't Jack. I doubt you called to reminisce about old times. So, what can I do for you?"

"I need your help. More precisely, I need your expert knowledge of drugs. Is possible to drug a person so that he appears to be dead without really killing him?" asked Anders.

"Yes, it's possible, but not with absolute certainty. To induce the appearance of death, the respiratory and cardiac functions of the person affected would have to be so reduced that the risk of actual death is equally as high as the chances of recovery. I don't recommend it. A situation would have to be pretty desperate for that tactic."

"It is. I have a guy siting in a Gestapo prison in Cologne. My man is under pretty high security. Obviously, I want to get him out. I'm hoping I can do so without having to resort to such desperate tactics, but I have my doubts."

"Emil Gottfried is head of the Cologne Gestapo. The man is a psychopath! They all are, but he's got a reputation for being extremely sadistic. Right up there with Heydrich.[15] His own men are terrified of him. If your man is still alive and has attracted Gottfried's personal attention, he would be better off dead. Personally, I'd kill him outright."

"Yeah, well, I want him out alive if at all possible."

"Then you will need help. I know just the person. His code name is 'Puffer' and he is also an excellent doctor. You will need a doctor to have any hopes of pulling this off. What you are proposing is very dangerous."

"Can your man meet me at the tavern on the west road outside of Düsseldorf tonight at 2100?"

Anders was to meet Goldilocks' man in the same area around 2200, so that would give him an hour to talk to Puffer and gather more information.

Cologne

Hogan had fallen into an exhausted sleep, though far from restful, shortly upon Gottfried's exit. Childhood horrors melded into adult terrors to haunt his dreams. He was six years old again and trapped in the discarded icebox into which he had hidden while playing hide-and-seek" with his friends. His screams of terror were unheard until the oxygen in the icebox was nearly depleted. He fell silent and passed out. The icebox materialized into a Gestapo torture cell containing the battered, nearly unrecognizable body of a man longing for a death that refused to come. The scolding voice of his father materialized into the insidious laughter of a sadistic Gottfried delighting in the eternal suffering of his helpless victim. Hogan awoke gasping for breath. The walls of his cell seemed to be closing in on him.

Stalag 13

The risk involved in any mission skyrocketed when that mission meant being out of camp in the daytime. Not only were they going out in daylight, but Gestapo headquarters in Cologne was 20 miles away which meant they would probably be gone at least a couple of hours. All of which added up to a pretty dangerous mission. Despite the fact failure would probably mean they could all end up in cells with the colonel, Carter had no problems finding enough volunteers for German guard duty. He had too many volunteers. If everything went well, no one but Carter and Newkirk would have to do any speaking. But just in case, they took the muscle men with the best command of the German language. Kinch was to stay back at camp. Aside from the obvious fact, Kinch's black skin would make it impossible for him to pass as a German; he was needed to man the radio room. LeBeau too was staying behind, and he was not too happy about it.

"LeBeau, I'm telling you for the last time," repeated Newkirk. "You're too small to be convincing as a Gestapo guard."

In a Gestapo uniform at five feet three inches, LeBeau looked more like a little kid than a seasoned soldier.

"Oh, I see, it's ok to be small when you need somebody to do the cooking, it's ok to be small when you need somebody to hide in a small place to listen in on a conversation, but it's not ok to be small when it comes to fighting. Well, I tell you, I'm as strong as any of you, and I can fight as well as any of you. I can be as vicious as it takes. Don't judge me by my size. Looks can be deceiving," shouted LeBeau angrily.

"I know that," replied Newkirk softly. "Hey look, Louie, I'm not the enemy. I believe you. In a fight there's nobody I would rather have by my side, but it's not a matter of what I believe, it's what the Krauts believe. You know how they are with their so-called 'master race'. Anybody not tall, blond, and blue-eyed is an inferior person. Look in the mirror, how many of those standards do you meet? Do really want to take that chance with the colonel's life?"

LeBeau looked down at the ground crestfallen. Newkirk was right and he knew it. He would have done anything for his colonel. He wanted desperately to do something — anything! That's what made staying behind so hard.

"And besides..." Newkirk put his arm around his friend's shoulder as he talked. "We need somebody to take care of things here, to keep the Krauts off balance. That's a pretty big job. The four of us are the only ones who really know how things run. Kinch is going to be busy in the radio room. And now tell me, can you really see Carter in charge?" The question got a snicker out of LeBeau.

"Oh yeah," replied LeBeau calmer, but not happier, "Why don't you stay and let me go?"

"Because my friend, it was my idea," proclaimed Newkirk.

* * *

"Now remember, don't speak unless spoken to and then say as little as possible. Let Carter and me do all the talking," instructed Newkirk as the truck pulled up to a stop in front of Gestapo headquarters in Cologne. The group got out and walked into the building as though they had done this all the time. With Carter and Newkirk leading the pack, they approached the corporal at the desk.

"I am Captain Dietz and this is General Franz. We have come to pick up the prisoner, 'Goldilocks'. Here are the orders," announced Newkirk, handing over Kinch's carefully prepared forged orders. With any luck very shortly they'd have the colonel back, then they could all laugh over exaggerated lies at dinner tonight.

"Ein moment, sir" replied the corporal as he picked up the phone.

"Sir, there are two officers here from Berlin with orders to pick up the prisoner 'Goldilocks'," explained the corporal to the officer on the other end of the phone. "Yes, sir. I understand."

"Colonel Gottfried is not here now sir, Captain Schmitt is in charge. He will be here in a moment," the corporal announced.

This was not good, thought Schmitt as he hung up the phone. If these men really were from Berlin, he could get in grave trouble for not turning the prisoner over to them.

Gottfried had made it perfectly clear before he left that he considered this prisoner private property and that he would tolerate no interference from anyone else. Those who displeased the colonel were taken into his private villa, never to be seen again. Nobody knew all the details of what happened in that villa, but the stories were pretty ugly.

"I am sorry, sir, but I can not turn the prisoner over to you without Colonel Gottfried's permission," replied Captain Schmitt.

"We have come all the way from Gestapo headquarters in Berlin. I demand you turn him over at once!" demanded Newkirk.

"Nein, I cannot. Not without orders from the colonel," replied Schmitt.

"You would…" shouted Newkirk.

"Ein moment," said Carter calmly, holding up his hand. "I am a general, a general out ranks a colonel, now I order you to turn over the prisoner to me."

Schmitt nervously replied, "I'm sorry, sir, but Colonel Gottfried ordered that no one but he questions this man."

"This is an outrage!" screamed Carter. "I am from Himmler's personal staff; the reichsführer himself wishes to question this man. He sent me to bring the prisoner to him. By defying me you would defy the reichsführer! Do you really want to defy Reichsführer Himmler?"

Schmitt swallowed hard, "No, sir."

"Good!" replied Carter "Now we are getting somewhere. Bring me the prisoner!"

"No, sir!" repeated Schmitt. He had seen Gottfried work, had seen the pleasure he took in an interrogation even after the prisoner broke. There was no doubt in his mind the validity of the stories concerning the fate of those taken to Gottfried's villa. He would rather take his chances with Berlin.

"Then I will talk to your colonel. Perhaps he will see reason, then I shall have you shot for insubordination!" screeched Carter, the veins bulging in his neck.

"He is at the fuel depot just south of here investigating an act of sabotage. I do not know when he will return," replied Schmitt.

"I shall return when Colonel Gottfried gets back and I promise heads will roll!" screamed Carter. "Come!" he ordered Newkirk, as he turned and stomped out.

"Coming, mein general!"

Newkirk's departing words to Schmitt were "I wouldn't want to be in your boots now."

* * *

Lang's thoughts were of happy times as a boy on the farm — of going out in the morning to help milk the cows, of summers, and of afternoons after school working in fields. He remembered his father's delight in planting and watching things grow. He remembered the smell of homemade bread and apple strudel from the kitchen, his mother singing as she baked and performed the household chores.

Then came the Great War. Oh, times were tough, but it was considered an honor to sacrifice for the fatherland, and besides, the war wouldn't last forever. Well, the war didn't last forever, but the effects of the war certainly did. Slowly the life which had brought such joy to his parents became a struggle for survival. Reparations for the war, everybody said. Cattle feed, supplies, and household goods became more expensive and hard to come by, while the price his father received for his goods at the market dropped. When they couldn't buy feed for the cattle, they tried to grow their own. But the land would not produce enough for the whole herd, so they reduced the size of the herd. Cattle sales didn't bring enough money to cover expenses, so they slaughtered the remaining cattle for food. After all the cattle were gone, they tried to live off crops from the land, but seed was impossible to get. In the meantime, the farmhouse deteriorated for lack of materials for its maintenance. By the time the family moved away to live with his aunt, the farm had deteriorated into a run down heap.

The struggles took a tremendous toll on his folks as well. The laughter and pride in his father's eyes was replaced by pain and failure. His mother stopped singing.

The fuehrer had put an end to the reparations and had rebuilt Germany. He had taken back the land Germany needed to support itself, started new industries, created new jobs, and had given the German people back their pride. Those barbaric allies weren't satisfied to have nearly destroyed Germany once. No! They wouldn't rest until Germany was in total ruins. They and their potato beetles and cattle plague, well, it would never happen, not if he could help it. Ernst Lang would do anything for the fatherland of his youth.

* * *

Anders and "Puffer," whose real name was Dr. Kurt Schell, were given the VIP tour of underground Stalag 13. Mike had to admit it was quite impressive —a machine shop, a wood shop, an electronics shop, a photo lab, a chemistry lab, wardrobe areas, a printing press, a kitchen, living areas, a communications room — he had seen bases with less complete facilities. And all right under the noses of the Nazis. Mike was astounded although he shouldn't have been. After all, Hogan had been an engineer before he was a pilot, not to mention a naturally creative person. He wondered if Wembley would consider Hogan such a "small loss" if he could see all this. Probably, Anders doubted Wembley's mind was big enough to comprehend anything bigger than a sheet of paper.

Anders noted the pride the men took in telling him about each part of the operation and relaying historical antidotes. A common thread in all the stories seemed to be Colonel Hogan said he wanted... and I/we came up with thus and such. This was the rare group that seemed to know the true meaning of the word "teamwork." Hogan would simply say, "I want this done," and would leave the men to use their own, not inconsiderable, skills to get the job done. With the proper motivation and left to their own devices, most of the men found they were capable of doing much more than they had ever dared to dream possible. This, in turn, inspired the men to accomplish even more. Hogan apparently was as liberal with the compliments and rewards for a good job as he was in passing out the work. The man knew how to motivate people, how to channel skills and energies into productive work and in return he not only got results, but also the undying respect and admiration of the people who worked for him. Anders could hear the awe in the voices as they filled him in on their operation. Mike noticed the continual emphasis on the word "our." "Our operation," as opposed to "Hogan's operation." Each man felt a certain degree of responsibility for the functioning of the unit. Along with pride, Mike could also hear something else in the voices — concern and worry. Worry about someone who meant a great deal to them. Well, that was why Mike was there.

* * *

Gottfried found a big charred patch of ground that in its former life had been a fuel depot. Interrogation of witnesses from the depot revealed that the fire had taken place shortly after a very careless cleaning lady had tried to clean the residue of an oil spill with bleach. The chlorine in the bleach had interacted with the petroleum in the oil to create a spontaneous combustion. With all that fuel oil around, it had not taken long for the heat generated by the combustion to ignite the fuel and totally destroy the depot.

Gottfried was infuriated! While hardly an act of sabotage, this imbecile's careless act had been very costly for the Third Reich. It had not only cost the fatherland a fuel depot when fuel was desperately needed for the war effort, it also delayed his interrogation of an important prisoner, a delay which could be catastrophic for Germany if the allies choose to initiate a offensive biological effort. This woman had to be punished. Suddenly an idea occurred to him, a way in which he could cut his losses. Gottfried ordered the woman be arrested and taken to his villa for "intense interrogation." Maybe this affair would not be a total loss after all.

Any fool could torture, mangle, or kill a person. That took no skill, but there was a real art to being able to inflict pain without causing damage. Knowing just how much a given human could take before passing out, inflicting pain just up to that limit, but not exceeding it, being able to inflict the maximum amount of pain for the maximum period of time — now that took real skill. Information could not be retrieved from an unconscious or dead person, but in general, given a sufficient period of intense suffering with no relief and no hope, the toughest person could be made to sell his or her soul. Like any art, the infliction of pain had to be practiced to maintain peak performance. This Goldilocks might prove to be a tough nut to crack. He couldn't die before he broke; too much was at stake. But Gottfried had a method. He could practice his method on this imbecile before he used it on the American.

She would pay for her foolish mistake and serve as an example of what happens to fools and enemies of the Third Reich. Emil Gottfried was a man to be feared — and obeyed!

By the time Gottfried reached the villa, his men had gagged and shackled the woman spread-eagle, face up to a table in his "playroom." *Like a human sacrifice* mused Gottfried with gee, *how appropriate.* Hmm, that was a thought. Maybe he would have an altar-type table built with an opening in the bottom for a fire, the heat from the fire below slowly cooking the person alive. Or, a table heated by an electrical current. However he ended up working it out, the slow roasting of a subject was an intriguing idea.

Gottfried's men were setting up movie cameras as he entered the room. The room contained raised platforms on either side for both cameras and their operators, designed so that the cameras had a clear view down on the hapless subject. One camera paned outward so that the subject's entire body would be in the field of view. The other zoomed in on the subject's face. Gottfried liked to study his interrogations. It helped him hone his skills. A lot of information could be gained about effective interrogation techniques from the body language of the subject during interrogation. In addition, it was just plain fun. Gottfried was a man who clearly believed in enjoying his work.

The woman, in her late twenties to early thirties, had the firm muscular build of a person used to hard labor. She was actually quite attractive. *This one might make a good addition to my trophy room,* mused Gottfried. Totally vulnerable, she lay still on the table, either resigned to her fate or too terrified to move. Gottfried walked over to the table and examined the face of the woman imprisoned on it. Once bright blue eyes, now red from crying, revealed the despair and the terror she felt. Feelings the voice longed to express were muted into barely audible, muffled sounds by the gag in her mouth.

Normally Gottfried didn't use gags. For one thing it was hard to get information out of a prisoner when the sounds were muffled and even, as the case was now, when there was no information to be gained, he liked to hear the screams and the pleading of his subject. They were reminders of the subject's powerlessness and Gottfried's power. But occasionally, depending on his mood, gags were useful — especially with women. Women's screams tended to be high-pitched, hurting Gottfried's ears. In addition, when bound and tortured, speech was the last thing a subject had control over. By taking away the subject's speech, the subject was totally and completely disarmed. It was the final tangible reminder to the subject of how completely and totally his or her fate depended on Gottfried's will.

Gottfried stroked the woman's long, silky, blond curls.

"Mmmmmm, mmmmmmm," she mumbled vainly trying to speak, eyes pleading, shaking her head as if to say "No."

He smiled as he caressed her face and neck — smooth, soft.

"MMMMMMM, MMMMMMM," she protested.

Gottifried ignored her, continuing to caress her. When he finally spoke, his voice was soft and reassuring as he wiped tears from her cheek and stroked her face. Torment was as much a part of an effective interrogation as inflicting pain. Toying with a subject's emotions, building the subject's hopes only to dash them, slowly chipping away at its resolve, eventually causing total demoralization. The effective application of torment was an art, which required much skill and practice. Gottfried was a skilled artist.

"You are frightened, my dear," he observed. "As well you should be," Gottfried continued while stroking her face.

The terrified woman whimpered through her gag.

In a heartbeat, Gottfried's manner turned icy cold.

Taking the woman's face firmly into his hands he asked harshly, "Do you know who I am?"

Terrified, the woman whimpered softly, acknowledging his words, weakly nodding her head yes, fear filling her face and eyes.

Basking in her terror Gottfried's hands moved slowly, tenderly to her neck as he gently caressed it. Then, to ensure her complete and total comprehension of his power, Gottfried slowly, methodically emphasizing every move, wrapped his hands around her throat and began to squeeze. He reveled at the life in his hands and his ability to snuff it out at will. Slowly, he squeezed until she began to choke, smiling as he did so, not releasing his grip until she was at the brink of unconsciousness. Only then did he let go. Even through the gag he could hear her gasping for breath.

"I am feeling particularly generous today. I will remove the gag and grant you the freedom to speak."

As Gottfried removed the gag, he asked, "Do you know why you are here?"

The woman replied weakly, still gasping, "I... I was... trying... to clean ... up a mess... and... and the fuel depot ... burned."

She paused catching her breath. Finally she fearfully, but firmly ask, "What are you going to do to me?"

In silence Gottfried let her observe his eyes look her over, head to toe, his face revealing pleasure with what he saw. Then he grinned an evil grin. Not missing the implication in his expression, the woman became agitated. She frantically shook her head, screaming, pleading.

"NO! NO! Please, no! Not this! Please, don't do this! I beg you! I am a good Christian girl… Don't do this to me! Please!"

Perfect! The imbecile thinks I want sex. How terribly naive! If she really thinks she's going to get off that easily, she is a bigger fool than I thought.

"You have committed a crime against the Third Reich and for that you must be punished!" proclaimed Gottfried harshly.

"I am truly sorry," she declared remorsefully.

"I meant no harm. I only wished to help. If I have done wrong, then punish me, as I deserve. Even kill me, if you must, but please, do not do this awful thing!" pleaded the woman, fear and desperation in her voice and tears in her eyes. "I am a good girl, believe me."

"Good girl or not, you have committed treason against the Third Reich. The penalty for treason is death." Gottfried proclaimed.

And die you shall, he mused, and then he smiled wickedly, eyes gleaming. *But not easily. In pain you will die. In long lingering, intense pain, and suffering, agonizing suffering such that you have never known. Such is the fate of those who betray the Third Reich. I, Colonel Emil Gottfried, will personally see to it. In pain and suffering, mine will be the last face you will see on this earth.*

"I have to prepare your punishment. In the meantime, contemplate your crime and enjoy what few precious moments of peace you have left. After that…"

His countenance was soft while he stroked her hair as if to comfort her, then turned vicious as he smiled.

"After that, you *will* pay for your crime."

I am personally going to take you on a journey through hell!

Gottfried smiled at her again, with that same hideous

smile that had nearly made Hogan melt. A smile that was so cold, so wicked it even made the blood of his own handpicked hardened men curl.

The helpless prisoner turned as pale as death. As Gottfried walked away, she began writhing and contorting as if to free herself from the chains binding her to the table, screaming and crying as she did so. Gottfried walked over to a cart against the wall and rolled it to the table. The contortions of the imprisoned woman were a sight to see. Gottfried paused to watch, beaming with sheer delight. There was nothing more exciting than a helpless, terrified subject struggling vainly to escape that from which there is no escape. She was definitely one for the trophy case. Gottfried noticed the cameras were on and rolling. Good, he would let them get this on tape before he got to work. Gottfried could only hope Goldilocks would be as entertaining when it was his turn. When this subject lay still, sobbing, exhausted from her struggles, Gottfried took two leads and connected them to the proper shots on the power supply. The other ends of the leads he attached to the subject's body. Gottfried did so gleefully, watching, feeling the chest rise and fall as she cried, once more, in awe of the life it displayed and his control over it. He remembered that he still needed her measurements. Gottfried carefully measured each part of the woman's body, savoring her terrified reactions as he did so. She rolled her head sobbing, begging.

"No. No, please no, I'm a good girl. Please, PLEASE, I beg you, don't do this to me. Pleasssse."

It was wonderful! The control, the power! If only Goldilocks weren't waiting, if only he had more time.

Once Goffried had finished taking measurements, he turned on the power supply. It had two controls: one for voltage and the other for current. High current killed, but high voltage with a low current was merely painful. He set the current low. For openers, he would use a low voltage and see how she reacted to it. He set the voltage and turned on the power supply. She jerked slightly, her muscles tensing and gasped. He noted her reactions were more indicative of discomfort than pain. Gottfried left the voltage on and continued to observe for a while, looking for signs that sustained application of voltage resulted in the body becoming tolerant of the effects of the voltage. He recorded his observations in a notebook. He increased the voltage slightly; the subject's muscles tensed more. She gasped again. Gottfried again recorded his observations, and then increased the voltage again. The cycle was repeated over and over. With each increase in voltage, her reactions became more and more pronounced. Eventually, the subject's body convulsed and she screamed in pain. In halting speech she cried,

"SSStop! … PPlease."

Gottfried made a note, "Subject's resolve weakening." He spoke not a word, but just smiled, an evil and haunting smile.

Not yet, my dear!

The cycles went on. The screams grew more and more intense, pain turning into agony.

"AHHHHHHHHHHHHHHH," she shrieked, her body convulsing in an ark with the table.

"SSSSTOP!" she stammered, "SSSTOP!"

Gottfried literally beamed, taking great delight in her anguished pleas to stop.

"Ohhhhh, … wwhy…" she stammered, laboriously "Whyy… aare you… ahhh… why are you ddoing… ohh… ddoing this… tto me?"

Silence. When Gottfried finally spoke, his voice was cavalier.

"It's fun!"

When the screams grew less intense, and the woman's eyes began rolling aimlessly in their sockets, Gottfried knew it was time to stop. He made a note of the current and voltage readings with an added comment, "Subject showing signs of shock." This was where the art came in, knowing when to stop. She couldn't lose consciousness, yet.

Gottfried slapped the semi-dazed woman on both cheeks a couple of times and let her rest a few minutes until she was fully cognizant of her surroundings. As Gottfried removed the leads from her body, the dazed woman groaned weakly, "Stop... no more ... please... kill me, ... but please... I beg you... no more! ... No more!"

At this point she would have done anything he asked to stop the pain. His experiment was a success! Gottfried was pleased, no, he was more than pleased — he was ecstatic. Goldilocks may have a higher pain tolerance. So for him, Gottfried might have to use higher voltages and adjust the cycles. Maybe even use more cycles. But this data provided him with some very useful information. Gottfried was confident the process would work equally well on the American.

Goldilocks would hardly qualify for membership in the master race, but he wasn't exactly ugly. Despite his dark looks, women probably found him attractive, and he no doubt enjoyed their attention. That would be his downfall, his weak point. That's where Gottfried would attack — his masculinity. The image of what a "real" man should be. A perceived assault on his masculinity would affect him the same way a perceived assault on her virginity affected this subject. Yes, it would work. Although Goldilocks put up a stoic front, Gottfried had caught the paling of color, even under the face paint, at his overture. Goldilocks understood the implication and it revolted him. Granted, the man's pride would not allow him to openly express his fear as the woman had, but Gottfried had seen it. It was a weakness that would work against him, which Gottfried could prey upon. Prey, as he suffered the agonizing effects of the electrical shock, the combination of pain and torment ever so slowly etching away at his granite like resolve until he broke. Then...

That evil look passed over Gottfried's face yet again. He could have done this for hours, even days. But fun as it was, this prisoner's usefulness had come to an end. It was Goldilocks' turn.

Gottfried stroked the woman's cheek reassuringly as he smiled sweetly letting her believe her punishment was over, that she would soon be freed, allowing her to recover, building her hopes, setting her up for the grand finale.

"Of course, my pretty, as you wish."

When she had settled down, her body ceased to quiver, relief flushed her entire being, he took his dagger, thrusted it forcefully into her left side directly under the rib cage, and left it lodged there.

"AHHHHHHHH!" she screamed, eyes bulging out of their sockets.

Her body instinctively tried to double up, but was held in place by the restraints.

Gottfried was a man who hated asymmetry, so he stabbed her again, this time under the right rib cage with the dagger's identical mate. There, that was better — symmetry! As she shrieked in agony, Gottfried looked down on her pain-filled face and smiled broadly.

Death you want, death you shall have. But on my terms, my lovely, not yours. And my terms mean more pain! Not an easy death.

Gottfried's mother had been a nurse. She had taught him about human anatomy and how to ease suffering. But through the Gestapo, Gottfried learned that the same knowledge which eased suffering could also be used to cause suffering — and that, to Gottfried, was much more enjoyable. He had learned his lessons well. The daggers lodged in the woman's sides would prevent the wounds from bleeding excessively outside her body, but they would not stop the internal bleeding. She would still bleed to death, but more slowly and painfully.

Gotfried groped his prisoner's pain-contorted body. He could feel its life slowly ebbing away. It energized him. The soft, pain-filled moans were music to his ears. It wasn't long before her skin became cold and clammy. Breathing was difficult and torturous. Each labored breath brought increased pain, the motion of the daggers slicing further into her body caused more internal damage, bleeding — and pain!

"Ohhhhh," she moaned. "My stomach… my stomach… ohhh… help me," she whispered breathlessly.

Blood began to fill the abdominal cavity. Gottfried noted her stomach was hard and distended when he touched it. She was weakening, the unbearable pain and blood loss driving her deeper into shock. The moaning woman began to weep softly.

"Help me!" she pleaded again, "Somebody… PLEASE… hhhelp me."

She paused.

"Ohhhhhh… the pain… the pain… ohhhhh … mercy," she whispered, her weak voice starting to trail off, "Have… mercy… ohhhh…hhhelpp… mme… pleeeeeeese! "

Her pleas for mercy fell on deaf ears. Gottfried was enjoying himself too much to have mercy on anybody. The men recording the event on the cameras were too afraid of Gottfried had they cared. Gottfried pressed hard on the swollen stomach. She shrieked so hard, Gottfried thought it would bust his eardrums.

"I'm so sorry, my precious, I'm afraid I'm just not in the mood for mercy,"

Gottfried replied with mock remorse, stroking her golden locks as she moaned softly, oblivious to his actions.

Gottfried mused that soon there would be a different Goldilocks for his amusement and wondered how much he would take before he too moaned in agony and begged for mercy. It would be wonderful.

Gottfried gleefully picked up the gag, twisted it and then shoved it in the dying woman's mouth, tying it tightly behind her head. In doing so, he took away her last freedom, her last hope, her last words that would never be heard. The very act itself assured her not only would there be no help and no mercy, but it denied her the means to ask for any, denied her an outlet for her pain, afforded her no comfort. Her last moments would be tormented, pain-filled, with only an apathetic cameramen and an uncaring tormentor for company. He saw hopelessness acknowledged in the woman's tear-filled eyes, in her whole face, racked with pain, intense pain and despair. How he relished the moment.

Gottfried knew shock when he saw it. She was starting to lose consciousness. Death would come soon. He shook her. Dazed eyes rolled in their sockets to look at him then closed; the body in his arms was going limp. He slapped her. She half-opened pain-filled eyes, and tried weakly to speak, her words lost forever in the gag as once more merciful darkness overtook her, this time never to lease its grip.

Gottfried shook and slapped her again. No response. She was still alive, barely. Gottfried embraced the limp form, as he absorbed the last flickering ambers of life from a body whose soul was now beyond his reach. Soon it was over. Well, she had been fun while she lasted. Now on to bigger and better things — Goldilocks!

* * *

"We tried everything we could think of, and I mean everything!" explained Carter as Hogan's men briefed Anders and Schell on the failed rescue attempt earlier in the day.

"Told him we were from Himmler's personal staff and that heads would roll if he didn't turn over the prisoner," added Newkirk. "Carter even tried to pull rank. As a general there should have been no problem, but instead that captain refused. He insisted nobody could have the prisoner without Colonel Gottfried's permission. When we asked to see Colonel Gottfried we were told he was away investigating a fire at a fuel depot."

Carter thought for a minute, "You know, that guy acted like he was more afraid of Gottfried than he was of Himmler."

"That would fit what we know about Gottfried," said Anders as he pondered the situation. "He's a pretty nasty fellow."

"We haven't given up. Kinch will call headquarters until he finds out when Gottfried is coming back. Then we go in and try again with this Gottfried," Newkirk explained. "We'll get the colonel back."

Anders pondered the information a moment then commented, "You can forget that. It'll never work. Gottfried is just plain obsessed with torturing Hogan. That being the case, he's not going to let him go to anybody for any reason. But the fact he is gone gives us a break."

Hogan's men looked at each other with puzzled expressions

then back at Anders as Kinch asked the question collectively on their minds, "How?"

"Simple," explained Anders. "Gottfried considers Hogan to be his passport to the big league therefore, he isn't going to let anyone else touch Hogan. That means during the time Gottfried is gone, Hogan is safe. We can use that time for preparation."

"Preparation for what? I thought you just said Gottfried wouldn't let the colonel out to anyone. If so, then how *do* we get him out? Or do you plan to get him out?" asked Kinch suspiciously.

"Oh, I plan to get him out all right, on a stretcher. Dead, he is of no use to Gottfried. A dead body should be pretty simple to get out."

Hogan's men were stunned by the remark. LeBeau was the first to speak, "You are going to kill Colonel Hogan!"

"In a manner of speaking, yes." Anders went on to explain, before Hogan's men could register any further protest. "I am, or more accurately, Dr. Schell is going to drug him, so that Gottfried and the Gestapo believe he is dead. Then a couple of you come in as ambulance attendants, carry him out on a stretcher (presumably for an autopsy), and bring him back to camp."

"You mean you're going to knock him out, tell the goons he's dead, and walk out of there with him just like that. You're balmy!" exclaimed Newkirk skeptically.

Schell spoke up, "It's a little more complicated than that. The truth of the matter is that we are going to poison him — Tetrodotoxin, or pufferfish poison known as fugu poison in Japan. It's a deadly toxin, but sufficiently diluted and carefully administered it can induce the appearance of death. Unfortunately, there is no guarantee that it won't actually kill."

"NO! You can't do that!" protested Carter, appalled by what Schell was proposing. "You can't kill Colonel Hogan!"

Anders responded, "I don't plan to kill him, not if it can be avoided. What the doctor is trying to point out is that nothing is one hundred percent foolproof and no matter how careful we are the possibility still exists that Hogan could die from the drug. With that in mind, we have three choices. First, leave him where he is and let him die by bits and pieces. That option has the additional risk that Hogan breaks and the Gestapo finds out about the operation here and makes further arrest and executions. Second, go in and kill him outright, clean and simple, no pain, no prolonged suffering. Would you rather do that? This option has the additional advantages that the Gestapo doesn't find out about the operation here. It buys us time to evacuate the camp and no one else suffers or dies. Lastly, the approach I have outlined here. Yes, I admit my plan could kill him, but the truth of the matter is the only way Hogan is coming out of that cell is on a stretcher and covered with a sheet. At least with my way he isn't tortured and he has a chance to live."

There was silence for a moment. Nobody wanted to kill Hogan. On the other hand, nobody wanted the colonel to suffer, nor did they want to do anything that would put the other prisoners at risk. It was a tough call, the kind of call the colonel himself would normally make except the colonel wasn't here. It was now their decision.

Finally Carter spoke up rather sheepishly, "Will..." he swallowed, "Will it hurt? The poison, that is." Everybody looked at him for a moment, bewildered. "I mean, he ends up dying anyway, how is being poisoned any different than being tortured? Heck, the Gestapo poisons people."

Furious, Newkirk got in Carter's face and began shouting,

"What? You are saying we're like those SS goons!? Why I ought to…" Kinch stepped in and grabbed Newkirk's arm before he could take a swing at Carter.

"I think Carter is concerned that the tactics we take trying to help the colonel might end up unintentionally being as brutal as those the Gestapo would take to break him," said Kinch.

Most of the time Carter was really goofy, but there were times when he hit the nail on the head. This was one of those times. If they went along with Anders plan and Hogan suffered and died as a result of being drugged, what made them any different than the Gestapo? The question haunted Kinch.

Schell explained, "I think the answer to Carter's question is 'no'. If the worst case scenario occurs and Hogan dies, he would suffer very little. With pufferfish poison the cause of death is generally suffocation. He might experience some discomfort, but he would feel very little pain. Pufferfish poison is very fast acting, so what little pain he would experience would be short in duration. I plan to give Colonel Hogan just enough poison so that, to the Gestapo, he appears dead, but not enough to actually kill him. However, where the respiratory and cardiac functions are concerned, there are never any guarantees."

"Are you saying he might simply stop breathing and die?" ask Newkirk.

"That's pretty much it, yes," replied Schell.

"Well, then couldn't you just do mouth-to-mouth resuscitation until he started breathing again?" LeBeau asked hopefully.

"Mouth-to-mouth would certainly be worth a try, especially if you can get him breathing on his own again right away. However, it can not be maintained indefinitely," explained Schell.

"Try me!" responded LeBeau defiantly.

"You know, I almost believe you could."

"Are you absolutely sure there is no other way?" inquired Kinch.

"Yes," replied Anders. "Believe me, I wish there were." *More than you know.*

"You tried yourself and you know how far that got. Anything else is only going to arouse Gottfried's suspicions and put others at risk. This is the only way."

"If it makes you feel any better, I wouldn't be participating if I didn't believe the situation was desperate. I definitely would never do anything to cause another human being to suffer needlessly," added Schell.

There was silence as each man became absorbed in his own thoughts.

"Sergeant Kinchloe, send a message on this frequency," said Anders handing Kinch a piece of paper. "Begin operation Papa Bear."

* * *

Now about this Goldilock's fellow... mused Gottfried. His experience the night before with the cleaning lady had excited him. At the end, she would have done anything he wanted to stop the pain — even assassinate the führer! He was quite certain he would find it true of the American as well. The man would tell him everything he wanted to know and then some. It was just a matter of finding the limits of his pain tolerance and wearing him down. The phone interrupted Gottfried's thoughts.

"Gestapo, Colonel Gottfried, Heil Hitler!" Gottfried bellowed into the phone.

"Colonel Gottfried, this is Major Hans Teppel of the

Abwehr. I understand you have a prisoner with some important information concerning the allied biological efforts. This could be a very big feather in your cap in Berlin. Congratulations! Good work! Have you gotten any information out of him?"

"Danke Major. No, I haven't gotten anything yet, but rest assured I will very soon," replied Gottfried puffed up.

"I have no doubt that you will," replied the voice on the other end of the phone, "but I need your help."

"What did you have in mind?"

"I have a man who is experimenting with a new foolproof technique for the interrogation of prisoners. The drug is a 'truth serum'. This drug will render a man incapable of resistance. He will answer truthfully whatever question you ask of him. I want to test this drug on your prisoner."

"NO! I see what you are after. You want me to send him to Berlin, so you can extract the information from him and take credit for yourself. No, I will not send you my prisoner!" shouted Gottfried.

Abwehr, or not, this Major Teppel could not have his prisoner! His electroshock technique would work. He, Gottfried, and he alone would get the information; then he would be a big man with Himmler. Himmler was the führer's right-hand man. Armed with Gottfried's information, Himmler would talk the führer into an offensive biological effort. After that, who knows where it might lead for him.

"You misunderstand me. I'm suggesting only that we help each other," Teppel touted. "I care nothing about your prisoner! I only want to test my drug. We can test the drug on your prisoner in his cell in Cologne. You may supervise if you wish. You will get the information you want and be a big man in Berlin. Afterward, you are free to do whatever you want with the prisoner."

Gottfried was suspicious. "Why would you be willing to give up credit for such important information?"

"If this drug works the way it is supposed to, I will be able to get whatever information I want from whomever I want anytime I want. I will have reliable information at will. That is what is important to me."

"And if it doesn't work?"

"Then you can interrogate your prisoner anyway you please and Berlin will never know about my failure. Either way we both win," Teppel was playing Gottfried.

"Will your drug harm my prisoner? I want him healthy for his execution." The truth of the matter was Gottfried had other plans and he needed him healthy, at least initially.

"No, it will not harm him. He will be perfectly healthy for whatever you have in mind for him."

Gottfried thought for a moment. *This man may have something. If this drug can get me the information I want, afterward, I could take Herr Goldilocks out to the villa and study his pain tolerances without having to worry about getting information. Just like with the woman.*

But unlike with the woman, Gottfried could take his time and really enjoy his study. He could make the man suffer for as long as he wished since low current electroshock did no physical harm. Suffer until his usefulness in that particular study was over and Gottfried got tired of him. *That might take a while, a long while* mused Gottfried with glee.

This man's eventual death would not be as quick or easy as the woman's. He would become the first subject in a new study, one aimed at determining the effects of anthrax on the human body. Gottfried would inject him with the anthrax bacteria. He would watch, as the man became sick and observe the symptoms displayed. At the height of his illness, Gottfried would dissect him — alive! From this Gottfried could determine firsthand how the anthrax had affected the organs.

"Send your man out."

Teppel's fish had taken the hook. "My man will leave Berlin right away. Dr. Ritter, accompanied by Captain Lambrecht from my staff, should arrive this afternoon."

"I will expect them then, Heil Hitler!" replied Gottfried. "Heil Hitler!"

* * *

The events of the past twenty-four hours had caused Tiptoe to be unusually reflective. Thoughts passed through his mind about how scared he had been when he was captured. He remembered feeling sorry for himself and wondered how a loving God could let a thing like this happen. Time passed, he was sent to Stalag 13, became acclimated to the camp, and got to know the other prisoners. As he listened to his fellow inmates, especially the European prisoners, he realized his life wasn't so bad after all. There were people much worse off than he was.

Tiptoe loved music, he loved people, and he loved God. He felt closest to God through music. He had gone into the ministry hoping that through music he could help others feel God's love as he did. During his time at Stalag 13, he had come to the realization that ministry wasn't music, although music could be a part of it. But ministry was loving and helping people. Stalag 13 had proved to be a rich gold mine of ministry opportunities. The funny thing about ministry, he was discovering, was that in helping other people you usually ended up receiving more than you give.

Another discovery Tiptoe had made was that ministry could be a very humbling experience. "Humbling" because there were always questions to which there were no earthly answers. For example, that night a month ago, Private Edward Henderson was an average airman. He had been born and raised in London, England, got married, and lived there when the war broke out. At the time of his incarceration, his wife was pregnant with their first child and he was looking forward to being a father. Like most prisoners, he had been demoralized over being captured and not being able to be with his wife and hold his daughter when she was born. But his wife sent pictures every week with a letter telling him every move little Anne made, like how much she was growing and how she looked forward to the end of the war, so she could see her papa. It didn't take Henderson long to become the reigning insufferable proud papa of camp. Last month in a cruel twist of fate, Anne had been killed in a German bombing raid on London. In her entire short life, Edward Henderson had neither gotten to see his daughter nor gotten to hold her in his arms. He'd never gotten to play with her or read her bedtime stories, and he had never gotten to tell her he loved her. Now all that was left of little Anne Henderson was pictures. Henderson was despondent when he heard the news. His friends were terrified of what he might do. They immediately sent for two people — Hogan and Tiptoe.

It had not taken Hogan long to size-up the situation and realize he was totally out of his league. This situation called for someone with counseling expertise and Hogan knew he wasn't qualified. Tiptoe, with his pre-war ministerial training, was the closest person in camp to a professional counselor. During the crisis, Hogan let Tiptoe use his quarters for private counseling in hopes that Tiptoe could get the bereaved private to settle down, at least enough not to do something stupid. Why would God let something like this happen to an innocent child? Tiptoe couldn't even imagine such a thing, yet there he was trying to help a man live with that very same tragedy. He didn't know what to say or what to do. He had no answers. Then he remembered something a wise professor had said once during a counseling class in the seminary, "You are young and think you have all the answers to all life's questions, but you will find, as you get into the real world, life isn't as black and white as it seems. You will find more and more questions to which you have no answers. When you do, pray! Let the person you are dealing with know you care, but above all pray! While you may not have the answers, God does."

All night long Tiptoe listened to Henderson. He cried with him, he hugged him, he prayed with him. When the two of them walked out of Hogan's office the next morning, Henderson was still depressed, that was to be expected, but Tiptoe was certain he wouldn't do anything drastic. Afterward, Hogan had made his quarters available to Tiptoe as needed for counseling with Henderson to help the man deal with his loss. Hogan, seeing the need for a private place where the men could go to discuss their personal problems, had gotten permission from Klink to set up a office for Tiptoe to conduct counseling sessions.

Tiptoe thought it was very generous of the colonel to give up his quarters for a grieving man. More than once since that night, he had wondered where the colonel had slept or if he had even slept at all. Until that night Tiptoe had dealt very little with the colonel. Most of what he had known about the man was from stories that floated around camp. Stories about a man who could escape anytime he wanted, yet chose to stay behind to help others get out of Germany. According to one story, Hogan engineered the escape of 20 prisoners all at once.[16]

Although never seen out of his role as an officer, Tiptoe had looked into Hogan's eyes when Hogan heard about Henderson's daughter and had seen pain for one of his men who was hurting. Hogan wanted to do something but was helpless. Then just as quickly, he saw the pain turn into anger. Anger at what he wasn't sure. Anger at the war? At the Germans? At himself? Whatever it was it had been intense. Maybe Hogan was feeling misdirected anger toward the Germans because he was really angry with himself for not being a superman. Anger at being human and as such limited in what he could accomplish. That last possibility concerned Tiptoe. Misdirected anger could be dangerous both for the recipient and ultimately for the person harboring it. Anger could eat a person alive. Tiptoe had seen a very compassionate soul in Hogan's eyes that night. He prayed Hogan wouldn't let himself be destroyed by unmerited self-anger. Hogan seemed to have much too much going for him; it would be such a waste.

The Colonel Hogan of the camp legends had given so much to help so many. The man in whose eyes Tiptoe had seen so much compassion and pain the night Henderson found out about his daughter certainly didn't deserve to be sitting in a Gestapo prison facing God only knows what. Why this was happening was yet another one of those unanswerable questions that was occurring more and more frequently, questions that increasingly drove him to his knees. Tiptoe said a silent prayer for the colonel. There was a rumor of another rescue attempt this afternoon. Tiptoe resolved to pray both for the colonel and for those involved with the attempted rescue until they successfully returned.

* * *

It had been over twenty-four hours since Hogan's capture. His future looked pretty bleak. Gottfried was a sadist. There was no doubt in Hogan's mind Gottfried's plans for him involved prolonged, intense pain. How long he could hold out before he cracked, Hogan had no idea. He only knew he had to hold out for the sake of his men. His other options were pretty limited, either make a break for it when the guards came and hope they would kill him out right or do the job himself.

In the Reserve Officers Training Corps (ROTC) courses he had in college, the instructors had told them if they had to commit suicide, do it right. Don't slit your wrist across the vein. Bleeding from slits across the vein can be stopped. Slit down the arm, down the vein. With the vein slit open lengthwise, no one can stop a person from bleeding to death. Easy enough. Surely he could find something sharp in this cell. Yes, it would be easy enough, but he couldn't entirely bring himself to believe the situation was truly hopeless.

Hogan's thoughts were interrupted by the sound of clanking at the door. *Well*, he thought, *this is it*. Sure enough, in walked Gottfried with two burly guards and two officers. The uniforms looked like Abwehr, but what were the Abwehr doing here? Then Hogan got a good look at the captain standing in the background. *Oh my... It can't be! He's dead!*

Mike Anders had not missed Hogan's look as he entered the cell. He had seen that same look many years before, in high school. There had been an old tree stump in his backyard. It was a royal pain to mow around. Its roots were too deep to dig up and refused to die. One day Mike decided to blow it up — gunpowder. It would be easy enough to make, all he needed was some charcoal, sulfur, and potassium nitrate. He had learned that in chemistry class. Charcoal, he had, potassium nitrate was nothing but saltpeter, no problem there. But sulfur... Mike decided to break into the chemistry lab one night and steal the sulfur. Nobody would miss it. The teacher would probably think the class had used it all in lab. Yeah, that's how he would do it. At night Mike reasoned his blonder-than-blonde hair would stick out like a sore thumb, so he put soot in it to make it look dark and not be seen in the darkness. That was when his troubles started.

Once inside the lab, Mike couldn't resist the urge to experiment a little, and, well, things happen. In Mike's case "the thing" ended up being a missing back part of the lab! As luck would have it — too bad he wasn't Irish — a teacher working late got a glimpse of him rushing away. Seeing the dark hair, she assumed he was Robert. A natural assumption, considering Robert was something of a mischief-maker himself, not to mention being about the same size and build as Mike. Robert was called into the principal's office the next day, along with his parents. Boy, did he get it! Robert's Irish luck had not helped him much that time. And his dad's Irish temper... even now the thought sent shivers up his spine. Mike felt bad. Just as he did now. He had not meant to get his friend in trouble. Mike caught up with Robert as he came out of the principal's office. Robert didn't say a word, just gave him that look. That same cold, hard icicle- dripping look.

Gottfried walked over to Hogan and smiled that same wicked smile that turned him to putty in their last encounter.

"My dear Herr Goldilocks these gentlemen are from the Abwehr. Meet Dr. Ritter and Captain Lambrecht. They are here to get the truth out of you."

"Have you ever heard of sodium pentothol?" asked the man Gottfried had identified as Ritter.

Although Hogan had heard of it, he remained silent.

"Sodium pentothol is a sedative introduced in 1936. When properly administered, a person is placed in a semi-conscious, hypnotic state in which he is totally incapable of lying," said Ritter matter-of-factly, partially lying himself. "Now lie down and roll up your sleeve."

Hogan knew resistance would only delay the inevitable; however, he was determined to make Gottfried work for his pleasure. As expected, the two burly brothers, as Hogan had dubbed them, threw him down on the cot and held him while the doctor pulled up his sleeve and injected him.

"Count backward from 100," ordered Ritter.

Hogan expected to become drowsy and was prepared to resist it. He had to maintain control of his mental faculties because too much was at stake. Over 100 lives depended on his ability to stay in control. He had to fight it!

"Tell us, who are you," a voice asked.

Silence. Hogan started to feel strange. There was a tingling sensation in his muscles. It started with the fingers, toes, and lips, then progressed to the rest of his body. He opened and closed his hands and flexed his feet, trying to make it go away, but it remained. A short time later, he began to feel lightheaded and dizzy, but not sleepy. *Boy, was it ever hot in here!* Hogan felt like he was in an oven. Perspiration poured out of every pore of his body. The tingling in his muscles worsened.

Hogan's throat and chest began to grow tight, as though encased in a giant hand with a death-grip slowly squeezing the life out of him. He vainly struggled for breath as breathing became harder and harder, his lungs refusing to work.

In the background he could hear baffled voices speaking in German, but Hogan was too preoccupied with the mutiny his body seemed to have launched against his brain to notice what was being said. Soon the tingling in his muscles stopped and numbness began to set in. He could feel his arms and his legs getting heavier and heavier. Movement was becoming increasingly difficult. Hogan felt his heart beating slower and slower and his breathing slowing and becoming shallower. The intense heat he felt earlier was gone; his body was growing colder and colder.

He was dying. Hogan knew it. He was certain by now his men had realized he was not coming back and, hopefully, had made their escape. Maybe they had even organized a mass escape to England, that is, if Klink hadn't realized he was gone and tightened security before they had the chance. Hopefully they had gotten away. But even if they had not, there was nothing he could do for them now, except die in silence.

Hogan regretted not having made provisions for his men in a situation like this. As a commander, Hogan was responsible for the welfare of his men, and in this, he had failed them miserably. He had failed them by getting himself caught. He had failed them by not having had an escape plan in case something happened to him. Just like he had failed a year ago when he had gotten shot down. Hogan never thought anything would happen to him, not really, therefore he made no contingency plans. His father had always told him he was a screw-up. Hogan never believed him until now. Hogan's father had never been able to hold down a job. Maybe that was why the old man had drunk so much, to numb the pain of being a failure. The Stalag 13 operation was Hogan's idea. He deserved whatever happened to him, but his men did not. They were only guilty of following the orders of a bad leader. At least with his death his men would be safe.

Gottfried had no use for drugs in his interrogations. He liked for his subjects to be fully cognizant of their helplessness, and to know that *he* was in control. Drugs tended to dull that awareness; they took away his power. Besides that, Gottfried felt drugs were terribly boring. Gottfried had heard of sodium pentothol. While Gottfried would have preferred to use his own methods of persuasion, he knew the drug would have no harmful effect on his prisoner. Once he had the information he wanted, Gottfried could give the prisoner lessons in control later.

Gottfried watched his guards hold the helpless prisoner down as Ritter (aka Schell) injected him with what he believed to be sodium pentothol. He saw the man's body relax as his struggle moved from the physical realm to the cerebral. Ritter asked a question. No answer. The prisoner squirmed, opening and closing his hands, rolling his head, obviously trying to resist the effects of the drug. *Hum*, thought Gottfried, *maybe this won't be so boring after all*. Before long the man turned pale and broke out into a sweat followed by labored breathing. This wasn't supposed to be happening. Something was wrong! Not that Gottfried wasn't enjoying his prisoner's struggles, but at worst sodium pentothol should have only put him to sleep. There was definitely something else going on here.

"This isn't supposed to be happening. What's going on?" Gottfried asked.

"I don't know. He seems to be having some kind of reaction to the drug," replied Schell.

"Isn't there something you can do?" Not that Gottfried was at all concerned about the man, he wanted information — and control!

"No, the damage has been done. All we can do is wait and see if he recovers."

"If!? What do you mean *if*?" shouted Gottfried in a rage. "Are you trying to tell me he is dying? This drug was supposed to do no harm to my prisoner and now you are telling me he's dying?!"

"Normally the effect is a harmless, mild sedation. There

are people who are allergic to the drug and have reactions, sometimes mild, sometimes severe, and sometimes fatal. Reactions are rare, fatal reactions even rarer. There is no way of knowing for sure if a person will react until the drug is tried. Apparently, this man is of one of those rare people," Schell lied, trying to convince Gottfried that what was happening was totally explainable, if unexpected.

The more Gottfried watched, the more convinced he was that his prisoner really was dying and the angrier he became. The prisoner's movements, breathing, everything, were weakening. His skin had taken on that bluish, cyanotic color of death. Gottfried realized the prisoner knew he was dying. He would never give Gottfried the information he wanted; nevertheless, Gottfried was determined to give the man that lesson in control before he died. Gottfried walked over to the dying colonel on the cot, jerked him up by the shoulders, and shook him viciously. Hogan's dying body barely reacted. Anders and Schell both watched in horror, helpless to do anything least they blow their own cover.

"You are dying, do you hear me?" said Gottfried to his severely weakened prisoner.

"Look at me," shaking Hogan again, "I am the last person, on earth you will ever see."

"Die knowing I am responsible, that your suffering gives me pleasure, entertainment, that I *enjoy* it!"

Gottfried embraced the body; he could feel the life draining from it. It was exhilarating! The weaker the prisoner grew, the more alive Gottfried became. In a last defiant act, Gottfried's prisoner made a very weak, minuscule attempt at a smile. His mouth opened very slightly and he made a feeble, unsuccessful attempt at speech.

Anders knew exactly what Hogan was trying to say. He

was trying to tell Gottfried, "Drop dead!" Anders had to bite his tongue to keep from telling Gottfried where he could go afterward and making sure he got there.

Gottfried felt the body in his arms go totally limp. In a rage, he threw it back upon the cot. There was no motion at all. Dull brown eyes stared, unblinking, unseeing, fixed on nothing, as lifeless as the body housing them.

Hogan's body lay as it had fallen, half-dangling over the side of the cot. Schell positioned him more comfortably. He took out his stethoscope, put it to Hogan's chest and listened. Then he reached over and gently closed his eyes. He looked at Anders and Gottfried and shook his head.

"He's gone."

"I will make arrangements for the body to be picked up," said Anders.

"What for?" replied Gottfried.

"Why, for an autopsy, of course," said Schell. "We have to determine why he died."

"YOU KILLED HIM WITH YOUR DRUGS!" screamed Gottfried. "You killed him before he could talk and now you want to steal the body!"

Was this man mad or what? Neither Anders nor Schell had expected Gottfried to battle over a dead body. Anders hated himself for what he was about to do.

"This man is of no use to you now. What good would keeping the body do? Why, this man was such a weakling he would hardly make a good trophy. Definitely not the hearty material of the master race. Look at him! One injection of a harmless sedative and he keels over. A good German would not have even blinked. Now tell me is the body of such a man (and you can barely call him a man) worthy of one such as yourself?"

Weak American, at least the cleaning lady from the fuel depot had the decency to plead for mercy as she was dying, thought Gottfried. Lambrecht was right. This piece of scum was hardly worthy his attention and now that his prize was gone (taking his information with him) Gottfried had much more important things to think about.

Schell reluctantly followed Anders and Gottfried back to Gottfried's office. Although he knew there was nothing he could do, the physician in him wanted to stay and look after his patient. One thing about pufferfish poisoning was that once in the system, there was very little anybody could do for the patient except wait it out. The next twenty-four hours would be critical. Until then, it was up to God and the colonel whether he lived or died.

Until today, Schell had never met Hogan, but during their brief encounter Hogan impressed Schell as being a man in whom lack of will was not a problem. While Schell had been appalled and shocked by Gottfried's treatment of a supposedly dying man, he had been equally astounded by Hogan's response, weak though it was. At that advanced stage of poisoning, Hogan should have been totally incapacitated. The fact he had been able to make any minute voluntary movement at all was nothing short of phenomenal. Yes, the man had a very strong will, which hopefully would transform itself into a will to live. If that were indeed the case, his survival would now depend on how cooperative God felt like being.

Inside Gottfried's office Anders made a call, supposedly, to arrange to have the body picked up and taken to Berlin. In reality, he was calling Kinch, who had tapped into Klink's phone line and was awaiting his call in the tunnel. Kinch in turn notified LeBeau, who was standing by with Sergeant Frank Wilson[17] and another volunteer, Corporal Walter Matthews, that it was time to move in.

As Schell and Wilson, the camp medic, had gone over Hogan's medical records the night before, Wilson had volunteered to accompany LeBeau as an ambulance attendant. Since Carter and Newkirk had been part of the earlier failed rescue attempt, Anders had decided to leave them at camp, lest someone in Gottfried's office recognize them and blow the whistle on the whole operation. It would be some time before Anders and Schell could rejoin the Stalag 13 group. Once again the physician in Schell was more at ease having Wilson on the "pick up" team. His presence would insure that Hogan would have access to some type of medical attention during the time Schell wasn't available.

Some time later the three entered Gestapo headquarters in Cologne.

"We have come to pick up the body of the prisoner to be transported to Berlin," LeBeau announced to the guard at the desk as he handed him a set of orders.

The guard looked at the orders, then replied, "Ein moment," as he picked up the phone. "Herr Colonel, three men are here to pick up the body of a prisoner they claim is to be taken to Berlin. All the paper work seems to be in order."

A pause.

"Jawohl, mein colonel."

"This way," said the guard as he led them down a hall into an unlocked cell.

It struck LeBeau as a little odd the cell would be unlocked, then he remembered, the colonel was supposed to be dead. Dead men have no need for locks. They can only go where they are taken.

Inside the cell, the colonel lay motionless on the cot just as Schell had left him — arms to his side, eyes closed. His dark hair was matted. Black face paint combined with sweat caked his face, which was covered by two days worth of stubble. There was dried blood on his cheek. Filthy Boche! What had they done to him? Tears welled in LeBeau's eyes. He couldn't cry now, later perhaps, but not now. Now he had to get the colonel out of this awful place, get him back to camp where people cared about him, where they could take care of him until he was better.

Matthews and Wilson carefully picked up the inert form and placed it on the stretcher. *Gee, he was cold! Had something gone wrong? Had the colonel really died?* They covered Hogan with a sheet, then carried him out to the ambulance and secured him in. Wilson and LeBeau got in the back with Hogan and Matthews drove off.

Once inside Wilson took the sheet off and began taking vital signs, *little if any pulse.* He had expected that. *Very faint heart beat and nearly imperceivable respiration.*

"How is he?" LeBeau asked anxiously.

"He's alive." *So far.*

LeBeau leaned over and whispered into Hogan's ear, "Don't worry, mon colonel, you are going to be all right. We are going to take you back to camp. A very good doctor is going to meet us there. He will take good care of you. We will all take good care of you. Don't you worry about a thing. You will be up and about in no time. You'll see."

As the truck sped away toward Stalag 13, LeBeau prayed he had not lied to the colonel.

CHAPTER 4
Goodbye Goldilocks. Welcome Papa Bear

Under the cover of darkness, the colonel was snuck back into camp. The dressing area had been converted into a makeshift hospital room. A solemn group transferred their stricken commander from the ambulance into the tunnel. The sight shook them to the core. Hogan's men realized the whole plan hinged on the fact that the colonel would appear dead, but they were in denial of its seriousness. They simply thought the doctor would knock the colonel out, bring him back to camp, some time later he would wake up and everything would be fine, as though he had taken a sleeping pill. Now the harshness of reality hit them squarely in the face and it was ugly. In the time they had known Colonel Hogan, he had always been a jovial, dynamic fireball of energy who could be in twenty places at the same time with a solution to every problem and an impish gleam in his eye as he planned the next caper. The cold, lifeless figure they had just brought into camp was a stark contrast to the man they knew. It hurt to see him that way.

"Is… is… he…" a teary eyed Carter choked on the words.

"No," replied Wilson to Carter's half-spoken question as they watched Schell set up an IV and take vital signs.

"What is he doing? What's that thing he is putting in the colonel's arm?" inquired an alarmed Newkirk.

Newkirk had a strong interest in medicine. His question stemmed partly from that interest, but just as much from a desire to get his mind off the morbid thoughts competing for his attention ever since he first saw the incapacitated Colonel Hogan.

"That 'thing' is called an 'IV' for 'intravenous' which means 'within a vein'. The solution inside the jar is saline."

"So what is he doing?"

"What the doctor is trying to do is raise the colonel's blood volume, thereby raising his blood pressure. He thinks there is a possibility the increased fluids might help clear the poison from his system faster.

"The way Dr. Schell explained it to me, this pufferfish poison acts as a paralyzing agent. It paralyzes the muscles of the body."

"If it just paralyzes the muscles, why is he so... so... dead?"

Wilson explained, "The heart and lungs are muscles. They are affected just as well as the skeletal muscles. Depending on the degree of paralysis, breathing slows and the heart rate, blood pressure, and body temperature all drop. If the lungs are sufficiently paralyzed, they can't take in air, so the person suffocates. Same with the heart. Paralyze the heart, and it can't circulate blood. Even if by some miracle the lungs could function, the person would still die."

Kinch joined the conversation, "What do you think his chances are?"

"I dunno." Pufferfish poison was new to Wilson; however, at the moment, he wouldn't have given the colonel much of a chance. Still, he had seen other men survive injuries he would have never thought they could. He had also seen men die when he thought they had every chance in the world of living, so right now he wouldn't dare venture a guess.

"Hey! Maybe if a beautiful, lady colonel kissed him, he would wake up," suggested Carter enthusiastically.

The men in the tunnel stared at Carter dumbfounded.

"What kind of a crazy idea is that!" ask LeBeau.

"Well, it worked for Snow White," replied Carter in self-defense.

"Snow White?" Newkirk repeated skeptically.

"Yeah, she ate a poison apple and the seven dwarfs thought she was dead. A handsome prince came along, kissed her, she woke up, and they lived happily ever after."

"Snow White is a fairy tale. People just don't recover from being poisoned by being kissed," chastised Newkirk. "Besides, where would you find a lady colonel?"

"London, and it has to be a beautiful lady colonel," corrected Carter. "We could radio London and ask tell them to send one."

"Excuse me!" exclaimed Newkirk with skepticism. "Are you *really* suggesting we radio London and tell them we need a beautiful lady colonel to bring our colonel out of a death trance? They would lock us all in a padded cell and throw away the key."

"Well, it wouldn't hurt. Besides, you never know."

"You know," Kinch mused, "Right now, I'm almost desperate enough to try it." *At least if he dies, he'd die happy.* Kinch was still being tortured by the question of what made what they had done any better than the typical Gestapo tactics.

After Schell had finished his work, LeBeau cleaned the colonel and combed his hair. Colonel Hogan had always been fastidious about his hair. LeBeau couldn't remember ever seeing him without every hair perfectly in place. Even when they woke him in the middle of the night with urgent calls from London, every hair was in place. LeBeau wasn't sure how he did it, or even why, but apparently well groomed hair was important to the colonel. If it were that important maybe, just maybe, having his hair combed would make him feel better. It made LeBeau feel better to do something no matter how trivial.

There is a law of physics called the *principle of the conservation of energy,* which states *energy may be transformed from one kind to another, but it can not be created or destroyed; the total energy is constant.*[18] It is the law by which a moving ball initiates motion in a stationary ball during a collision. As Schell made it clear there was nothing anybody could do but wait, each man tried to go about his own business, finding all kinds of excuses to stay in the tunnel rather than go to bed. Carter puttered about the chemistry lab. Newkirk discovered that the costumes desperately needed his attention. LeBeau busied himself in the kitchen. Kinch decided it would be a good time to catch up on all the work that needed to be done in the radio room. But the four men found themselves drawn back to that dark, cold room, each absorbed in his thoughts. As though just by being there, they could initiate life in the body of the silent figure lying on a cot, in the same manner a colliding ball initiates motion in a stationary ball.

* * *

Andrew Carter had been raised on a farm in the rural town of Bullfrog, North Dakota where everybody knew everybody else, everybody trusted everybody else, everybody helped everybody else, and locks on houses were unheard of. As a result, he lacked the worldly exposure the others had. He was naive partly by nature and partly by upbringing.

Carter was the oldest child in his family. He had watched how his friends' older brothers taught them things and looked out for them. Many times Carter wished he had an older brother too. Because of his expertise in explosives, upon arrival in camp he had been asked to join Hogan's men. There he found not one, but three big brothers. Yeah, they picked on him and yelled at him sometimes, but it didn't bother him. That was what brothers were supposed to do. His friends' brothers had always acted that way. Besides, sometimes he really was a screw-up. He couldn't learn if he wasn't corrected and that was just their way. Carter knew that when the chips were down, the guys would be there for him.

And then there was Colonel Hogan. Colonel Hogan was the daddy of the group. Ok, maybe not the daddy. After all, he was only ten years or so older than they were, but sometimes it was hard to think of him as an officer. Officers were formal. They made you salute, shine your shoes, and stand at attention. Colonel Hogan wasn't like that. As long as you did your job and did it right, that was all that mattered. The best part was Colonel Hogan didn't tell you how to do your job; he just let you do it. And boy, could he come up with the ideas! The colonel was, well, — the colonel. He looked out for them, he joked with them, he needled the Germans openly, and he sabotaged the Nazis covertly. In Carter's mind, he was a hero right up there with the Lone Ranger.

The coloring of Hogan's skin disturbed Carter. He had never seen anybody look that blue before. Well, that wasn't quite true. His Aunt Edna had looked like that before she died. And she really wasn't his Aunt Edna. She was his Great Aunt Edna, his father's aunt, but he called her aunt. Aunt Edna had been old ever since Carter knew her, older than dirt. She had been sick for many years before she had died. In the world

Carter knew, only old, sick people died, and Colonel Hogan was not old. He wasn't sick, not really. It was the drug that made him sick. In couple of days it would wear off and he would be fine. Once again he would be a living dynamo of energy, bouncing around, coming up with crazy ideas, and giving orders. Anyway, that was what Carter wanted to believe.

* * *

Newkirk had been outside in the compound that day in November of 1941 when the truck drove up. *Looks like more prisoners,* he thought grimly as he strolled over to check out the situation. The Krauts already had France. England was all that stood in Hitler's way to world control. Judging from the rate at which the Krauts were taking prisoners, even that wall would fall before long. To his astonishment the truck contained only one person.

"Welcome to the toughest POW camp in all Germany," Newkirk yelled to its sole occupant.

Before the man had a chance to reply, Schultz herded him into Kommandant Klink's office. Newkirk didn't recognize the uniform. *Hmm,* he thought, *maybe I'd better check this out.* A few minutes later Schultz and the "unknown soldier," exited Klink's office and headed toward the cooler. Newkirk made a point of tripping and bumping squarely into the man, lifting his wallet in the process. Looking into the wallet as Schultz left with his charge, Newkirk read, "Colonel Robert E. Hogan, United States Army Air Corp, serial number 0876707." An American, now what was an American doing in Germany?

"Hey, Schultzy! Who's the VIP?" Newkirk asked, catching Schultz as he exited the cooler.

"He's not a VIP, he's a new prisoner. An American officer, Colonel Hogan."

"Aw, come off it, the Americans aren't even in the war. Who is he really? Gestapo? Come on Schultzy," taunted Newkirk pulling a candy bar out of his pocket and waving it in front of the bulky sergeant's face as he leaned over and spoke softly into his ear, "You can tell me. Who am I going to tell?"

"No! It's for real. The Kommandant says Americans have been flying with the RAF for months now."[19]

"Oh yeah, is that so?" replied a skeptic Newkirk, "So, what's he doing here? This is an enlisted man's camp. Why isn't he being sent to an officers' camp?"

"Maybe the Kommandant likes him. I don't know. The big shots don't tell me everything," replied Schultz as he took the candy bar from Newkirk and walked away.

If Schultz were right, then this was too good to be true. If the Yanks were entering the war, even on a limited basis, maybe there really was a chance to keep Hitler out of England. In the meantime, officers got certain perks. If this colonel really was going to be a permanent fixture around Stalag 13, it might be to Newkirk's benefit to get into good standing with this guy. *That shouldn't be too hard to do. A little flattery here, some buttering up there, a piece of cake! After all he's an officer, how smart can he be.*

"Hand it over, Newkirk, or I will mop up the floor with your eyelashes."

As it turned out, Hogan had been pretty darn smart, smarter than Newkirk ever imagined a human being — especially an officer — could be. He not only recognized Newkirk's brush with him on his first day in camp as a pat down, but he also designed their complex tunnel system and engineered what would become the most bizarre rescue and sabotage operation of the war. Newkirk's thievery and tailoring skills earned him a place among the elite in Hogan's operation and gave him a chance; he thought he would never again have to defend his native England against the Nazi monsters. For that, Hogan would always have his undying gratitude and his loyalty.

* * *

It was ironic that LeBeau was now fighting tears and standing vigil over a man that just a year ago he wanted to kill. To say that Hogan and LeBeau didn't exactly hit it off on their first meeting would be the understatement of the war.

"You know that could be construed as giving aid and comfort to the enemy," Hogan said when Newkirk introduced him to LeBeau and explained that LeBeau had a talent not only for cooking, but also for making friends with anyone, Krauts included.

LeBeau would have strangled Hogan then and there with his bare hands had Newkirk not intervened and kept him from doing so. This arrogant American had some nerve calling him a Boche lover. What do Americans know about war anyway? Sitting back in their nice warm houses, not wanting to get involved, analyzing who is doing what to whom as though it were a game of chess. They would be singing a different tune if the bombs were raining on Washington or the Boche armies were marching into New York. It would be an entirely different story if it were their relatives being rounded up and executed by the Gestapo.

"I hate them!" he finally said, in a voice so low he could hardly be heard. "All of them. I'd rip their throats out for a centime. But for now I make them like me, and someday, when they don't expect it, I'll find a knife sharp enough to cut an onion... or a Boche..."

And hate them he did. He hated them with a passion that

went beyond words. He hated them for what they had done to France, but most of all he hated them for what they had done to his family. They had forced his mother and sister from their homes and worse of all, they had killed his brother. Pierre was only 16. He was as big for his age, as Louis was small, with a passion for life and a feeling of indestructibility that only a youth can have. In some respects Pierre had been very much like Carter. He had that same innocence and that same kind heart. They had great fun joking about the contrasts between their sizes and their ages. Louis may have been older than Pierre, but at six feet three inches and a muscular 240 pounds, Pierre could have crushed Louis with one arm. One of Pierre's favorite things in all the world to do had been to run up to Louis, yell "Big Brother!" and wrap his arms around him, pick him up, give him a big bear hug, then toss him into the air. It never bothered Pierre that Louis was small. On the contrary, he idolized his "big brother." He always said, "good things come in small packages," and Louis was "the best." Pierre's adoration made Louis feel like he too was six feet three.

Pierre followed Louis into the army; Pierre told them he was 18. Because of his size they believed him. After the German occupation of France, he joined the Free French, "to liberate France from the tyranny of the Boche swine," he had said. But Pierre's big heart had been his downfall. He had mistaken an undercover Gestapo agent for a fellow Frenchman in need of help, and Pierre had paid with his life. LeBeau had just gotten word of Pierre's death two weeks before Hogan's arrival at Stalag 13. His wounds were still raw. Hogan's remarks concerning his loyalty just rubbed salt into them.

But despite their first rough encounter, Hogan's mind had started to work, and when it worked things happened. He had foreseen LeBeau's culinary and social skills as being a a method by which to get information from the enemy. LeBeau too had earned a place among Hogan's small, but efficient group, and the chance for vengeance in ways he would have never dreamed possible. LeBeau would gladly give his own life if it would save the life of the man who had given him the chance to fight the filthy Boche pigs that had destroyed his world.

* * *

Kinch's thoughts were interrupted by the sounds of somebody entering the tunnel.

"Hey! I won't touch anything. I promise!" yelled Tiptoe as he raised his hands and kept them clearly in sight and clearly away from anything mechanical or electrical in the tunnel.

Despite the grimness he was feeling, Kinch chuckled, "That's all right. Actually, I'm really glad to see you. Right now, your prayers are worth more than all the equipment in this camp. Equipment can be replaced."

"Sergeant Kinchloe," Tiptoe began, "I wish I had a direct connection to God. If I did, I would be back in Tennessee feasting on good ole country cookin' instead of the mess here." Kinch chuckled as Tiptoe continued softly, "The truth is, ministers are here for the people on earth. They have no more of a direct connection with God than anybody else. My prayers as a minister don't mean any more to God than yours. God loves us all. That's why he sent Jesus, to break down the barriers resulting from God's perfection and man's imperfection, so we can talk directly to him. God *wants* us to talk to him directly, no middlemen, no barriers, except the ones we erect ourselves and even then, he can remove them if we ask."

"Yes, I know, but your prayers are still welcomed."

"That's what I'm here for," replied Tiptoe as he walked into the room where the colonel lay.

Kinch understood Tiptoe's words more than Tiptoe would ever know. His father was a circuit riding Methodist preacher. He had taught his son the Bible, about God's love, and prayer. That is, when he was home which wasn't often enough. There in had been the problem. Being a preacher demanded long hours, very little pay, and twenty-four hours availability — and Ivan Kinchloe had resented it! If God were available twenty-four hours a day, why did his father have to be too? God didn't need his father's help. Why couldn't his dad take him fishing instead of running to Widow Warner's house every time she thought she was having a heart attack and was going to die? Why, she was as healthy as a horse! Everybody knew she just did it for attention. Why couldn't his dad play ball with him rather than go to the hospital when old man Magee had gallbladder surgery? The doctor could get along fine without his dad under foot. The more time passed and the less Ivan saw of his father, the stronger his resentment grew.

Ivan did everything he could to be different from his father, not that he was openly rebellious. His rebellion was subtle in nature. It would manifest itself as involvement in activities that had little to do with religion: from prize fighting to working for the phone company. In doing so, Ivan gradually grew away from the God that had demanded all his father's attention. Grew away, until the day his plane was shot down over Germany. Suddenly he realized how very much he did need God, especially if he were to survive. For the first time in years, Ivan began to pray. And he found out that God does answer prayers, even those of a backslider who had no use for Him. It was true that God had not answered his prayers the way he wanted. If he had, Ivan would be sitting at home by a nice warm fireplace instead of freezing in a tunnel under a POW camp but, Ivan was alive. And thanks to a certain creative American colonel, Ivan had a chance to really make a difference.

Ivan had not stopped praying since the colonel left camp. He knew God heard his prayers and would answer then in His own way in His own time. Still, he found Tiptoe's presence and his added prayers to be a comfort. Even though ministers were flesh and blood, human beings like everyone else, and — like Tiptoe said — had no more influence on God than the average person, there was an inexplicable sense of peace and reassurance that came from having a man of God present — and praying! Maybe the whole thing was psychological, but for whatever reason it was there. James Ivan Kinchloe suddenly came to a new understanding and appreciation for his father. He hoped that someday he would have the opportunity to discuss his newfound knowledge with his father and ask for his forgiveness.

* * *

Tiptoe didn't have the faintest idea what to expect when he walked into the tunnel. He had heard all kinds of rumors ranging from the colonel was back, but hurt, to he was dead. He suspected the truth lay somewhere in between. Whatever the case, he felt he was needed, which bought him to his problem — how to break the rank barrier? Sure he had dealt with, even ministered to, officers that outranked him. But the officers he had dealt with since being interred at Stalag 13 — which was where his ministry had really begun — were non-commissioned officers. Hogan was a commissioned officer and a high-ranking officer at that! There was a big difference. His experience with commissioned officers had been limited to "Yes, sir" or "No, sir." He didn't have a clue how to deal with an officer in need.

Walking into the room, Tiptoe saw a man lying on a cot. Without his uniform and rank insignias, Tiptoe saw Hogan for what he was — a human being. A human being more dead than alive, but alive nevertheless. His problem was solved. Tiptoe did what he would do for any person in the same position. He walked over to the man, sat down next to him on the cot, and took the man's hand in his.

"Colonel, I don't know if you can hear me or not. If you can, I want you to know you've influenced a lot of lives inside this camp and a lot of lives outside of this camp. Lives you may never know about, touched in ways you may never know, but touched just the same. I hope you don't mind if I say a little prayer for you.

"God, we thank you for this man and for all the good he has done. In the brief time I've known him, I've seen the concern he has for those in his charge. I've seen how he cares for them. I've seen the sacrifices he makes for the benefit of others so that they may see their homes and their families again. God, I don't believe that your work for his life is done. I ask that your healing hand be upon him. That you will surround him, protect him, and give him your strength and peace. I also ask that you be with the ones who care for him. There are so many who care. Give them your strength and peace also. In Christ's name, amen."

Hogan heard Tiptoe's words just as he had heard everything. Despite his appearance, he had never lost consciousness. He had been totally lucid from the time the needle was placed in his arm to the present. Back in the cell, totally convinced he was dying, Hogan found Gottfried's temper tantrum amusing. Gottfried would never get the information he wanted, nor would he get the perverse joy of torturing Hogan. The last laugh, quite literally was Hogan's.

Gottfried knew it and Hogan knew it. By the time Gottfried flew off into a rage, Hogan's body was so numb Gottfried could have done anything to him and he would have never felt it. It came as a complete shock that his body made any response at all when he tried to tell Gottfried to drop dead. But the even greater shock came upon hearing Schell pronounce him dead.

No! No! He tried to scream. *I'm still alive! I'm not dead yet!*

By that point his mind had lost all control of his body and it frightened him. Hogan now observed life without being a participant. This totally contradicted all his expectations of death. He had expected to be over taken by darkness, a total lack of awareness, a sleep from which he would never awaken. The whole nightmare made Hogan think about his childhood.

As a child his parents had made him go to church. He didn't like it because it was boring. He had to sit still too long listening to boring lectures when he would have rather been out playing. At the age of four, a Sunday School teacher told his class that they would be studying God's creation the following Sunday. She asked them all to bring something from nature to show the class. The following week Hogan found a baby black snake. His mother would have killed it, and him too, if she had known he had it. He very carefully kept it hidden in the garage until Sunday then took it to church. Miss priss Cindy Longsworth nearly had a fit! She screamed, ran around the room, and tried to climb a bookcase, pulling it over on top of her in the process. She wasn't hurt, but the teacher was scared to death! She jerked Hogan up by the ear and told him if he didn't straighten up, he'd burn in hell when he died. If being a prisoner inside your own body forever wasn't hell, he didn't know what was. But the teacher had been wrong about the burning bit.

On the other hand, maybe she wasn't. What if they cremated him? What would happen when his body burned? Would he feel pain? Right now he couldn't feel anything. But he could see, or at least he could until Schell closed his eyes, and was aware of everything that was going on. What would happen to that awareness if they burned his body? Would that part of him burn too, would it feel the flames? Worse, what if they buried him? He would be trapped in a tiny little coffin, just barely big enough for his body, under the ground forever. The thought alone terrified him beyond description. It would be just like when he was trapped in the icebox, except while inside the icebox his body functioned. There was just no room for him to move. What if he had not been pulled out unconscious, just moments away from death? What if he *had* died? At the point of his death would he have awakened like he was now, unable to make his body move, aware of everything going on around him? And now, thirty years later after his body had decayed, where would his soul have been? Still in the casket? Still aware of his surroundings? Would he forever be a terrified little boy with awareness but no body? Right now he was a terrified adult with a useless body. Moreover, terrified as he was, he couldn't feel his heart racing. That terrified him even more. A racing heart would have at least hinted he was alive. It seemed there was no comfort to be found anywhere.

It wasn't until the guys showed up and Wilson began working on him in the ambulance that Hogan finally let himself believe that just maybe he wasn't dead after all. It was LeBeau's reassurance that gave him any hope at all his mind and body would work in unison again.

Hogan was not a particularly religious man, but the past few hours he had existed in a living hell. He wished Schell had not closed his eyes. Hogan's near fatal childhood experience had left him severely claustrophobic and subject to massive panic attacks in surroundings the least bit confining. Down in the darkness of the tunnels unable to see, he found his old nemesis, claustrophobia, working against him. As long as he could hear something, voices, movement, anything he was fine, but the minute it became silent (trapped inside his body, blind, unable to move, barely able to breathe) panic set in. Hogan found Tiptoe's words comforting. Strangely enough, afterward, Hogan had felt the most peaceful he had had since this whole affair began. Miraculously, even the panic attacks subsided.

Thanks, Hogan thought.

With the panic attacks gone, Hogan's mind was free to think about other things like the officer in the cell. The one Gottfried had called "Lambrecht," but everyone in camp was calling "Anders." Anders sure looked a lot like his childhood friend Timothy. As teenagers Timothy and Hogan had hung around together. They had three common interests — horseback riding, motorbikes, and girls, not necessarily in that order. Where girls where concerned, between the two of them, the other boys never stood a chance.

Timothy and his twelve brothers and sisters were as American as Hogan; however, their German parents had taught them to speak German like natives. It had driven Hogan crazy! Not that he cared to eavesdrop on their conversations, but because Timothy insisted Hogan speak it as well. In retrospect, Hogan had Timothy to thank for the fact he had known enough German to converse with the local town's people to get assistance setting up the Stalag 13 operation. Except, Timothy had died in an airplane crash in 1938. Or had he?

* * *

Unlike Hogan's men, Anders was having a difficult time staying in the same room with the man. After all, they had not been responsible for putting the needle in Hogan's arm, he had.

Mike had always been something of a thrill-seeker, so was Robert. That was one of the common traits the two of them shared that made them friends. They use to sneak out on Robert's father's motorbike for a ride. While Robert's thrill was in the ride itself, Mike's had been in the covertness, the challenge of sneaking without getting caught. It was thrill-seeking that led to the chemistry lab incident which nearly destroyed their friendship. In retrospect, the stump had not been that big a problem. It was just a challenge, a challenge sitting there day after day, daring Mike to do something about it. Even then, Mike could have broken into the chemistry lab, taken the sulfur, and left with no one being the wiser. The truth was, alone with all those chemicals, Mike couldn't resist the urge to play around and see what would happen when various chemicals were mixed together.

Mike's parents taught him to take responsibility for his actions. As a result, when the principal and Robert's dad came down hard on Robert, Mike felt so bad, he confessed. His parents grounded him for a month, but the worst part was Robert wouldn't even talk to him. He just glared at him with that look of his, the one that dripped icicles. Finally, Mike managed to talk his dad into lifting his curfew long enough to find Robert, apologize, and hopefully set things right again. Mike knew exactly where to look. Robert loved planes and dreamed of flying. Not too long before, he had talked a local businessman, Emmett James, into hiring him as a motorcycle courier for his airplane-based courier service in hopes of eventually working his way into a pilot's position. Mike found Robert getting ready to go on a run.

"Hey look, I said I was sorry. I told Mr. Higgins I was the one who blew up the lab and you had nothing to do with it. What more do you want?"

Robert gave him a hard look and went over and put his pouch on the motorcycle. At least it wasn't dripping icicles. That was a step in the right direction.

"Come on, Robert! Chew me out if it'll make you feel better. Just talk to me. Say *something!*"

"Drop dead! There you happy?" replied Robert angrily.

"Come on, Robert. I didn't mean to get you in trouble. We've been friends too long to let this come between us."

"You didn't mean to get me in trouble. HA! That's a laugh!" snorted Robert. "You don't know the half of it. Do you know where I was while you were blowing up the school? I was here."

"Here? I thought everything closed after 7:00."

"It does. After my last run, Mr. James said he wanted to talk to me. You know what we were talking about, my future — college! Yeah, college. Mr. James thinks I should go to college. Me, whose family hasn't a nickel to its name. And even if I saved all the money I ever made on this job, I could never afford to go. Mr. James told me about a program the Army has called ROTC. He even offered to help me get into it. And you know what else, he said if I continued to work hard and stay sober, he would teach me to fly when I turned 18. Do you know how long I've dreamed of learning to fly?"

"That's great!" Mike exclaimed, excited for his friend.

"It was until that chemistry lab thing," said Robert more calmly now. "I don't know how Mr. James found out, because I certainly didn't tell him, but somehow he did. He went and talked to Mr. Higgins and told Mr. Higgins I couldn't have possibly had anything to do with the chemistry lab blowing up because I was with him at the time."

"I still don't understand why you are upset. That should have gotten you off the hook."

"Oh, it did at school, but that was how my parents found out I'd been riding Dad's bike and working for Mr. James. Then the whole roof caved in at home. When Mom found out I'd been riding Dad's motorbike, she about had a cow. Dad wasn't exactly thrilled about it either. Not only that, Dad nearly blew a fuse when he found out I'd been working for Mr. James. Dad never liked Mr. James, especially since Mr. James fired him for being drunk. He didn't like me working for him either. Told me to quit. He said Mr. James was a loser and only losers worked for losers. If I continued to work for him, I was a loser too."

"So what are you going to do?" a concerned Mike asked.

"Keep working of course."

"What about your folks?"

"Aw, I'll deal with them," replied Robert trying to display a confidence he did not feel.

And that was that, or so Mike thought until several months later. There was this girl, Vicki Austin, that Mike had really liked. She was a real beauty: tall, a knockout body, dark hair, dark eyes, and intelligent too. Mike had tried for months to get a date with her, but she refused to go out with him. "Not my type," she said. Finally, after months of hard work and charm he won her over, and she agreed to go to the prom with him. He was so excited. At long last, a date with Vicki Austin. That was all he could think about the whole week before the prom. On the day of the prom Vicki called to say she was sorry, but she was sick and couldn't go. Mike was disappointed, but sick was sick, and one couldn't help being sick. There would be other times. He went to the prom stag, certain he'd pick up somebody before the night was over.

About an hour after he arrived, in walked Vicki on Robert's arm. Robert looked over at Mike and smiled smugly. Mike knew this was payback for the chemistry lab incident. Robert didn't just get mad, he got even.

That same love of adventure was the reason Mike joined the OSS. At first it had been fun. He loved the covertness: spying, stealing secrets. But somewhere along the way reality began to set in. Mike had lied to people he loved. He had hurt people he loved, innocent people — like his family. Sometimes, the people he hurt were not so innocent. People died. Anders himself had killed a few. *For a higher cause* he told himself. But along the way, black and white had muddled into shades of gray — like Hogan. What if he died? Although deep down Mike knew he had done the right thing, he didn't feel good about it. Mike found himself wondering what kind of a man he had turned into. *What kind of man would poison his best friend?*

* * *

It was a worried Ernst Lang that made his way to the villa that night. The man, Goldilocks, had died without giving up any information as to the allied biological program. Well, not quite, He had said that the allies were planning to drop bombs of potato beetles and cattle plague on Germany. The effects could be as devastating, if not greater, than the reparation demands of the last World War. A chill went up Lang's spine, but not from the cold. Lang knocked on the door of the villa. A servant answered. He was bundled up in a coat, scarf, and gloves. It was clear Lang had caught him on his way out.

"I'm Ernest Lang. I'm here to see Colonel Gottfried."

"The colonel is in the study. Down the hall, the last door on the left. You can't miss it."

"Danke."

As Lang approached the end of the hallway, he heard a woman's screams. It made him nauseous. This was obviously another of Gottfried's interrogations. While Lang didn't approve of the Gestapo's methods, times were desperate. Desperation forces people to do things they wouldn't ordinarily do. The allies had to be stopped before they destroyed Germany. Ernst would do whatever he could to help. To Lang's horror, he found Gottfried engrossed in a film of a previous torture session. His staring eyes wide open, glistening with delight and madness. His mouth turned up in a wide smile, his face exuberant. The screams Langhad heard were from a terrified, tortured, humiliated woman chained to a table with two daggers in her sides — Greta! A very pale Lang raced from the room. Once out the door he kept on running. He had to get as far away from that God forsaken place as fast as he could. In the meantime, Gottfried was too engrossed in his perverse enjoyment to even notice.

* * *

As the dawn broke, Anders had to run Hogan's men out of the tunnel to roll call. When the last man climbed over the railing and the bunk closed, Anders motioned for Schell to come out of the make-shift hospital room.

"Ok, now tell me the truth. How is he really."

"He's alive. He's been stable for over twelve hours now. That's about all I can say."

"That's it? Surely, there's something else you can tell me."

"Well, if it helps most deaths usually occur within six to eight hours of poisoning. He's well past that marker."

"Then he's going to be all right?" ask Anders anxiously.

"I can't say that. People have been known to die as long as twenty hours from the time of poisoning. I won't be able to say for certain until it's been at least twenty-four hours. But I can say this, every hour he lives increases the odds in his favor. If he's still alive tonight, then I can be fairly certain he'll recover."

Returning to his patient, Kurt Schell reflected on his first experience with pufferfish poison. Schell had just finished medical school and felt like doing something exotic. He and a good friend decided to visit Japan. While there, they learned of a Japanese delicacy called "fugu." Upon inquiring, they were informed that "fugu" was the Japanese name for pufferfish. Fugu contained a very deadly poison called tetrodotoxin which is found mainly in the liver, gonads, intestines, and skin of the pufferfish. Tetrodotoxin is so deadly, that for pufferfish to be served in a restaurant, chiefs had to be specially trained and licensed to carefully remove the organs containing the toxin, thus reducing the danger of poisoning. Despite careful preparation, fugu poisoning was still a common occurrence in Japan.[20]

Being forewarned, Schell wisely decided fugu was something he could live without. However, his friend wasn't so wise. One night the friend decided he wanted to try fugu. Nothing Kurt said could talk him out of it. After a couple of bites he began to complain of being weak and dizzy. Schnell took him to the hospital where he developed the full symptoms of severe fugu poisoning. Despite all Schell and the Japanese doctors could do, a few hours later he died. Grief-stricken, Schnell was leaving the hospital to make arrangements for his friend's body to be shipped back to Germany when a Japanese doctor stopped him. According to the doctor, in Japan it was a custom not to perform any burial preparations on a person who experienced fugu poisoning until three days after the individual's poisoning. The doctor went on to explain that sometimes respiration and cardiac functions become so suppressed even trained medical personnel can't detect them. Yet, once the poison begins to wear off, the vital signs return to detectable levels generally within three days.

Kurt dismissed it as Japanese superstition. He was a doctor. He knew death when he saw it and his friend was dead. However, to humor the old doctor he agreed to wait three days. After all, one couldn't be deader than dead, so what would three days hurt. Within twenty-four hours, his friend's heart was beating and he was breathing again. Kurt could hardly believe it! In less than a week, with the exception of some residual muscle weakness, his friend was fully recovered and swearing off seafood forever! Schell was horrified to learn that throughout the whole ordeal his friend had been totally aware of everything going on around him. He had even wanted to punch Kurt in the nose for trying to bury him.

For Kurt the experience generated an interest in pufferfish poisoning. The Japanese loved pufferfish so much, it was a shame eating it had to be so dangerous. Kurt began to research tetrodotoxin. His rational was the more he knew the better treatments he could design, thereby reducing the danger. Schell never dreamed his knowledge would be used to intentionally poison a man. He had misgivings from the start about using the toxin in this operation, but unfortunately he had also seen the results of Gestapo interrogations. Any lingering doubts in his mind about the necessity of the poisoning had been quickly dispelled by his encounter with Gottfried.

* * *

A grief-stricken Lang pondered the events he had briefly witnessed the night before. *Why?* He thought. *Why Greta? She certainly wasn't an enemy of the Third Reich. She didn't have any secrets vital to the war effort. In fact, she didn't have any secrets at all. She was so sweet, so trusting, so innocent. Why?*

Lang had known Greta all her life. Her parents had owned the farm next to his family's. Their families helped each other with the sowing and harvesting of crops, so they had grown up working the fields together. Lang was embarrassed to admit Greta could work rings around him, for she didn't seem to mind hard work. Greta was a beautiful girl not only on the outside, but inside as well. She never saw the bad in people. That trait left her open to be taken advantage of. Lang reminisced on their teenage years.

Ernst Lang had reached the age when he was starting to notice girls were different from boys and was appreciating the differences. Greta, although younger, was physically maturing early and rapidly becoming a head-turner. Ernst wasn't the only one who had noticed. Several boys in town were paying her quite a bit of attention. She loved it! It wouldn't have bothered Ernst, except these guys were rougher boys, not exactly noted for being gentlemen. One day in town Ernst overheard them talking about her as though she were a piece of meat and placing bets as to which one of them would "score" first with her. Ernst saw red! He told them in no uncertain terms to stay away from Greta and gave them a piece of his mind. In turn, Ernst received the worst beating of his life and a warning to mind his own business.

"You had no right to treat my friends that way," exclaimed Greta furiously when she found out about the incident.

"Greta, they are not your friends, they just want your... ah... Well, they want something from you and when they get it, you'll never see them again."

"If that's the case, then all they have to do is ask. I'll gladly give them anything I have."

She was so unselfish; the concept of unscrupulousness was foreign to her. *Oh boy,* thought Lang. *What have I gotten myself into? Oh well, facts are facts and Greta needs to know the facts, so here goes.*

"Ah, sit down. Let's talk." She sat, down watching him intently. "Ah… let's see… ah… I don't quite know how to say this," Ernst stammered in a big brotherly fashion.

"Yeeees?" Greta replied mischievously, her bright blue eyes still watching him intently, not letting him off the hook.

"Well… ah… Have your parents told you about the facts of life?"

"Sure, they said I'd grow up meet somebody special, fall in love, get married, have babies, and raise a family."

"Ja, well, there's a little more to it than that. Between the getting married and having …"

"Ernst Lang!" she shouted jumping up, putting her hands on her hips and glaring at him angrily. "How dare you! I would never do a thing like that! I'm a good girl! How dare you even suggest such a thing!"

Whew! At least she knew.

"I know you are a good girl and I know you wouldn't. But you are a very pretty girl and there are boys out there who like pretty girls, but they like them in a bad way, a selfish way. These boys are bad boys and they don't care if a girl is good or not."

Greta looked at Ernst impishly, "Are you a bad boy?"

"Of course not!" exclaimed Ernst indignantly. "I would never do anything thing to hurt you or anybody else."

"Then how do you know they would?"

"Because… because," he really didn't want to say it. He didn't want to be the one to crush her innocence, but she had to know. For her own good. "Because I heard them talking about it."

"You… you… *heard* them?" her voice was broken and she was near tears.

"Yes, Greta, I heard them." Ernst got up and put his hands on her shoulders. "Greta, you are a wonderful, kind-hearted human being, but you've got to understand that not everybody in the world is like you. Some are, but some care only about themselves, but most are somewhere in between."

She hugged him as she started to cry. "Please, don't cry. Just promise me you'll be careful. And remember, if you need me I'll always be there."

If you need me I'll always be there. I'll always be there. I'll always be there.

The words haunted Lang like a broken record. The words as well as the glance he had gotten of Greta's dying moments and the expression of perverted glee on Gottfried's face in reliving that moment made him sick. So why had he not been there? Why had he not known she had been arrested? Why didn't he stop it? Why did she die tortured and tormented at the hands of a deranged, unfeeling killer with no one to defend her? Why, because he was too busy living in the past, nursing a grudge against the allies for his family's misfortunes during the great depression following the First World War. Because he had been too absorbed in anger and self-pity to see Gottfried or the Gestapo for what they truly were. He had wanted to believe that the Nazis were the saviors of Germany, the white knights in shining armor. He had closed his eyes to the truth. Now Greta had paid the price. The man in the cell had been right. They were monsters.

I would never do anything thing to hurt you or anybody else.

More haunting words from the past. What about the allied agent? Did he have a wife, children, sisters, brothers, parents, people who cared about him? What kind of person had he been? In the barn he seemed to have a good sense of humor. Lang realized he didn't even know his name, just a code, Goldilocks. What about *him?* He had told Greta he would never do anything to hurt anyone else and now the man was dead. Killed by the hands of the same man that killed his beloved Greta. What was worse, Lang had lured him there. That made Lang as responsible for the death as if he himself had put the needle in the man's arm. Was somebody somewhere suffering the same grief over this man Ernst was grieving for Greta? Was he really any better than the Gestapo? Was he any better than the British or the French, just because he had believed he was doing the right thing at the time? Maybe the British and the French governments had thought they were doing the right things when they made reparation demands of Germany. Life had suddenly become very complicated.

* * *

The past few days had taken a toll on everybody. Hogan's men had done what was necessary to keep things going in camp and prevent the Germans from suspecting something was up. Now when their presence wasn't required above ground, they were below — watching and waiting. Schell carefully watched the colonel's vital signs.

With only a week and a half until Christmas, Tiptoe double-upped on tree practices, which also served as prayer meetings. He also organized a round-the-clock prayer vigils. In addition to whatever prayers the men made privately, they also signed up for specific times in which they would pray for the colonel, insuring that he was prayed for at all times during the critical twenty-four hours of his illness. In this time, Tiptoe had made frequent trips down below encouraging and praying with the colonel.

In spite of the crisis underneath the camp, there was an overall positive effect going on in the camp, the result of which was an epidemic of good will and bonding among the inmates of Stalag 13. Men who had never prayed before began praying and found an unexpected positive effect on each of their lives as well. Most found a sense of peace not previously experienced, as though a large weight had been lifted from their shoulders. All the men in camp began to share prayer requests and pray for each other as well as for the crisis under the camp.

As the twenty-four hour mark passed, the men breathed sighs of relief. With the crisis behind them, Hogan's men began looking for signs of life returning to the colonel's body. While the men refused go to their own beds, over in the night Schell observed that each man had found his own separate corner and sacked out, exhausted by the events of the past two days.

Kurt Schell smiled as he took his next set of vitals. Respiration and heart rate were both slightly higher than they had been over the past twenty-four-plus hours. After what seemed like an eternity, the poison was finally beginning to wear off.

"Hey guys look!" shouted a jubilant Carter upon waking the following morning, "He's breathing! He's breathing!"

"He's been breathing, you clod," replied Newkirk. "You just can't tell it."

"No, I mean you can actually see him breathing!" Carter retorted.

"Carter's right," exclaimed an equally excited LeBeau. "His color is better. That bluish tint is gone. He actually looks human now. More like he is sleeping than dead."

"Guys," Kinch nodded toward the radio room suggesting they move the conversation there.

"What's wrong?" asked Newkirk.

"What's wrong is that he's probably hearing every word you are saying. Come on, think about it, how would you feel listening to a bunch of guys carrying on about your breathing and color."

"Oops! I forgot about that," exclaimed Carter.

"He can chew me out all he wants to," replied LeBeau. "It will be music to my ears."

"Yeah," mused Newkirk," I never thought I'd see the day when I'd look forward to a bailing out by an officer. Still, Kinch is right, we need to be more careful what we say."

It was a more cheerful group that leaped over the railing to roll call than had gone out any morning in the past three days.

"Why don't you go get some rest? I'll stay with him," Anders told Schell as the last of Hogan's men left for roll call.

"Ok," replied Schell. The colonel was out of danger now and he had not realized how tired he was. "But call me if there is any change."

"Will do," replied Anders with a smile as he walked Schell to the exit of the room, "and thanks!"

"I didn't do anything. It was him and God. They did it all."

"Yes, but they couldn't have done it without you. Good night or rather good morning!"

"Good whatever!" replied Schell with a yawn.

A short time later, Anders saw the fingers on Hogan's hands begin to twitch.

"Timothy," Hogan whispered, barely audible.

Anders sat on the cot next to Hogan and took Hogan's hand in his. "Yeah, Robert, I'm here. Relax. Take it easily. I know I've put you through an ordeal, but it's over now, you are going to be fine and the name is Mike Anders. Remember that. Timothy Sonntag is dead. I'm Mike Anders. I will explain everything when you are feeling better and we can talk alone. I promise. Now get some rest."

Hogan weakly shook his head, then dozed off into the first peaceful sleep he had had in over two days.

Mike Anders, formerly known as Timothy Sonntag, smiled and watched his friend sleep. There was no doubt Robert would hold him to his promise of explanations. But Mike also knew he wouldn't talk. Just like he had not talked about the chemistry lab incident. Although Robert knew, to this day the teachers and principal would have never found out if he had not told on himself. Robert was not that kind of person.

* * *

For the third morning in a row, Tiptoe fell out for roll call in Colonel Hogan's place. By now it had just gotten to be a habit. Schultz noticed and was not happy.

"Where is Colonel Hogan?" It's been three days and he is nowhere to be found."

"Ok, Schultz if you must know," Newkirk began, "Colonel Hogan has gone on a little vacation. He'll be back."

"Vacation! Vacation! Prisoners are not allowed to go on vacation. He has escaped!" shouted an agitated Schultz. "I must report this to the acting kommandant."

"Relax," said LeBeau, "The colonel has not escaped. He will be back in a few days."

"Yeah," interjected Carter. "The colonel can't escape."

"Oh yeah, and why can't he escape?" asked Schultz sarcastically.

"Because he'd be in a lot of trouble if he did." Carter rambled on, "The escape committee voted down any escapes by officers. And when those guys say 'no' they mean 'no'. You don't mess around with the escape committee. We enlisted guys can escape anytime we want to, but officers, no way."

"Oh, so Colonel Hogan can't escape because he's an officer. What kind of a dummkopf do you think I am?"

"Schultz," replied Kinchloe, "didn't your mother ever teach you not to ask embarrassing questions?"

"I'm not asking embarrassing questions. I'm asking 'Where is Colonel Hogan'?" shouted an exasperated Schultz.

Newkirk sighed, "I'm afraid we've going to have to tell him, mates. Don't tell anybody, but Colonel Hogan is really a spy. He went out the other night to meet another agent and was picked up by the Gestapo. We had to poison him to get him out. Since then he has been lying in a make-shift hospital room in our secret tunnel until he gets well which should be in, oh, a day or two. You can come see him if you like."

"Jolly joke! I can see the colonel right now and he is standing right here. Right Colonel Hogan?"

"Absolutely!" replied Tiptoe.

"You say he'll be back in a day or two?" Schultz whispered to Newkirk.

"Sure, end of the week at the most."

"End of the week?!"

Kinch interjected, "Colonel Hogan will be back by the time Kommandant Klink gets back."

"Schultzy, would we lie to you?" ask LeBeau.

"Ja."

"True, but we aren't this time," interjected Kinch again.

"But you just said you would lie to me, so how do I know you aren't lying when you say you aren't lying?"

Before any of the others could reply Tiptoe spoke up.

"I'm a minister, right?"

"Jawohl."

"Ministers don't lie, right?"

"Ja, at least they aren't suppose to."

"Well, then, if I tell you, that Colonel Hogan will be back by the time Klink gets back will you believe me?"

"Maybe."

"Will this help my credibility?" asked Tiptoe pulling a candy bar out of Hogan's pocket.

"You are a minister and ministers don't lie," proclaimed Schultz taking the candy bar from Tiptoe's hand.

"All present and accounted for!" exclaimed Schultz as Roth appeared from the Kommandant's office.

"Very good, carry on. Dismissed!"

"Hey! That was pretty good," said Carter to Tiptoe as they entered the barracks.

"Just because I'm a private doesn't mean I'm stupid," replied Tiptoe. "Does all this talk about the colonel coming back mean he's getting better?"

"Well, the critical mark passed yesterday afternoon," Kinch explained. "Schell said sometime in the night his vital signs started improving. This morning his breathing and color were better. When we came up for roll call, he was still paralyzed though. According to Dr. Schell, when the poison starts wearing off, improvements should come rather rapidly. He says that with the exception of some residual muscle weakness, he should be up and about in a couple of days. Even the residual effects should clear up within a couple of weeks."

"That's good news. I think this camp could use some good news," replied Tiptoe.

It was a noisy group that made their way into the tunnel.

"Hey, you guys want to hold it down. We've got people sleeping down here," Anders said to the group as they came down ladder.

They looked around and saw Schell asleep on the cot in the radio room. The guy must have been exhausted. He had stayed up with the colonel ever since they had brought him back to camp. Kinch didn't have the faintest idea when the last time was he had slept before that. Like most of them, he had been up most of the night before the rescue making preparations. He was a most thorough man. It could have well made the difference between Hogan's living and dying.

"Sorry, we're kind of wound up. How's Colonel Hogan?"

"Good," responded Anders. "He's finally starting to come out of it. While you guys were gone he moved a little and tried to talk to me."

"What did he say?" ask Carter.

"He couldn't quite get it out. I told him to relax and promised to fill him in when he was feeling better. Then he nodded off to sleep."

LeBeau headed out the door.

"Hey, where are you going?" Kinch asked.

"To make chicken soup. He hasn't been able to eat for a day and I doubt the Gestapo fed him. He is going to need some food."

"Louie," Newkirk began, "For over two days we've been trying to keep him alive. Don't go killing him now."

LeBeau muttered something in French and headed off to the kitchen. Anders chuckled.

"Ah, you understand French?" Newkirk asked inquisitively.

"Only what I learned from high school," Anders responded.

"Well, what did he say?"

"You don't want to know."

Hogan slept most of the day. LeBeau pumped him full

of chicken soup later when he awoke. He was very weak. He couldn't sit or feed himself. He could barely speak, but he was living and that was the important thing. The rest would come later.

"How do you feel?" asked Schell

Hogan replied weakly, "Like death warmed over."

Schell laughed, "I'd say that's a fairly accurate assessment. If it makes you feel any better, the worst is over now. You should find your strength returning fairly rapidly. Take it easy and get as much rest as you can. It will make your recovery easier."

Hogan dozed off and on throughout the night. Each time Hogan awoke LeBeau would fill him full of chicken soup. It was amazing how much strength he seemed to gain each time he awoke. Schell claimed it was the poison wearing off, but LeBeau knew it was his chicken soup.

Although still weak, by morning Hogan was able to sit, speak, and move unassisted. Facts which delighted him to no end.

"LeBeau, how about changing the menu?" Hogan complained when LeBeau came in with yet another bowl of chicken soup. By now Hogan felt like he was drowning in chicken soup.

"What, you don't like my cooking?" a hurt LeBeau replied.

"Colonel's grouchy this morning. It must mean he's getting better," Newkirk interjected. "I don't blame you for complaining about the food though."

LeBeau made a face at Newkirk.

"Pipe down, fellas. LeBeau, I love your cooking."

"Oh, that there is a sick man," exclaimed Newkirk.

Hogan gave Newkirk a look of long suffering and

continued, "I love your cooking. It's the chicken soup I don't like."

"What's wrong with the soup, mon colonel?"

"Nothing, the first hundred times, after that it loses something."

"Then I will cook you a meal fit for a king!" exclaimed LeBeau excitedly.

"Don't worry about the 'fit for a king' part just make sure there is no chicken in it," ordered Hogan.

"Oui, mon colonel" replied LeBeau as he made a hasty exit. A short time later he returned with a breakfast of eggs, bacon, and toast all cooked to perfection. LeBeau was true to his word; it *was* fit for a king. Hogan had to admit it was the best meal he had eaten in days. In reality, it was the only meal he had eaten in days, not counting the gallons of chicken soup LeBeau had poured down his throat during the night.

Hogan was finishing his breakfast when Anders entered the room. "How are you feeling?" he asked.

"Better than I've felt in awhile," Hogan answered truthfully.

"Good. Dr. Schell has gone to town for supplies and everyone else has gone to roll call. We are alone. Do you feel like talking?"

"No, I feel like listening. Listening to you explain what this is all about. Why you faked your death." One thing about Robert, he always got right to the point.

"As you know with thirteen kids in the family, I couldn't afford to go to college. The military route you took didn't appeal to me, so I got a job with a car dealership. In the mid 30's some of our more well-to-do customers became interested in the German Mercedes. By that time, I had worked my way up in the company. The fact I spoke fluent German and knew something about the customs, made them decide to send me to Germany to negotiate a deal. Afterward, I acted as a liaison. It worked out pretty well for me. I got to see the country of my parents' births and the relatives I had only heard about from letters. Of course, the best part was I while I was there, I managed to negotiate a great deal on a motorbike, a BMW R-12, for myself.

"During my negotiations with Mercedes, I had worked with a New York international trade lawyer who later became an OSS operative. When things heated up in Germany and the OSS began serious recruiting for their German operations, he remembered me. As a result, I was offered a position. Because of my German-American background, I was a natural. I could pass myself off as German and nobody would ever know I wasn't born in Germany. You know me; I love anything covert, so I jumped at the opportunity. At the time it sure beat selling cars. I made one mistake, though," Mike said sadly. "I never should have shipped my BMW home. If I had any idea I was going to end up spying, I never would have. But, I couldn't have it shipped back over here without blowing my cover," Mike sighed deeply. "Too bad, it was a great machine. I sure do miss my BMW."

"My BMW," Hogan corrected.

"Yours?" Mike looked puzzled.

"Yeah, mine," Hogan grinned. "Your dad gave it to me while I was home on sick leave after you 'died'. He said none of the other kids got into biking the way we did. He thought you would have wanted me to have it. And you are right, it is a great machine."

Mike snickered, "Yeah, Dad called it right. I guess the old man knew me better than I realized. At least you can appreciate it for the wonderful machine that it is. So what happened? I thought you were a die hard Indian fan."

"Well, ah..." Hogan fidgeted nervously. "I ... ah, ... I changed my mind."

Mike stared at Hogan in confusion for a second then he smiled a broad smile as the light suddenly dawned.

"You wrecked it! You, the grand master of all that flies on earth or sky, wrecked your Indian. Oh, ho!" Mike laughed, "That's one for the history books."

"Oh yeah, I'd like to see how you do on black ice!" retorted Hogan defensively.

"Black ice, that's nasty stuff. Just what were you doing on black ice?" Mike paused for a moment, "You said sick leave, how badly were you hurt?"

"Just a broken ankle and some scrapes," Hogan admitted, not mentioning the concussion.

The accident happened in November of 1938. The last thing Hogan remembered was riding into what he thought was a puddle across the road while on route to a date. When Hogan, who was always very prompt for dates, failed to show, his date, a gorgeous redhead named Francis, became concerned and started searching for him. When she found him he was sprawled in the middle of the road, unconscious with what was left of the bike on top him and his leg twisted underneath him. Two days later he awoke in an army hospital, sick as a dog with his ankle in a cast. He was told he had hit a patch of black ice.

Hogan continued, changing the subject, "You still haven't explained why you faked your death."

"Do you remember my Aunt Bertha and Uncle Karl who came visiting one summer?"

"Yes, but what do they have to do with why you faked your death?"

"They have everything to do with it. You see, between

both of my parents, I still have quite a bit of family in Germany, Aunt Bertha and Uncle Karl included. If the Nazis ever found out who I really am, it wouldn't be any trouble at all to track them down. Once located, the Gestapo could have my family arrested as hostages or kill them in retaliation."

"So you faked your death and created a new identity to prevent the Gestapo from tracking down your family."

"Yes."

"What about your parents, your brothers and your sisters? They were really heart broken when you 'died'." Hogan recalled the hurt in Timothy's father's voice the day he gave him Timothy's bike.

"Not telling them has been the hardest part. You may not want to believe this, but just as we have spies over here, the Nazis have spies in America. Word from America could get back here just like that," Mike replied snapping his fingers. "Besides, how do you think they would feel if they knew about what I was doing? Trust me they are better off thinking I'm dead."

Hogan thought about his own mother's reactions about his learning to fly. She never forgave Emmett James for teaching him. He could understand very well why Timothy had not wanted his family to know about his occupation. Hogan leaned back against the wall and closed his eyes. Despite all the squabbles, Timothy and his family had been close — much closer than Hogan had been to his. Hogan suddenly realized how much Timothy — Mike, he was going to have to get use to calling him 'Mike' — had risked to save him.

"Robert, are you all right?" Mike asked with concern.

"Yeah, fine. Just tired, that's all."

"I'm sorry, I didn't mean to tire you out. Get some rest. We can continue this later."

"No, I'm fine," Hogan replied curtly. "I want to continue this now. Look, I know who you are, who you were. I'm grateful to you for getting me out, but in doing so you've revealed to me the fact you aren't dead. I'm here in a German prison, free for the taking whenever the Nazis please. How do you know I won't talk?"

"It's a risk. But life is about risk. Besides, I know you too. You didn't talk after that chemistry lab incident and you were furious with me then. I don't think it's likely you would talk now. Besides, we work in different circles. The odds of the Germans even putting the two of us together enough to *want* to press you for information about me are pretty small."

There were a million things Mike wanted to ask Hogan about, his family: how they were, what was going on in their lives, maybe even rib him a little about the accident, but although he would never admit it, Mike could see that Hogan was growing fatigued. The poison still wasn't completely out of his system and he needed to rest. Hopefully there would be more time for talk later.

"Roll call will be over soon and your men will be coming back, so we better draw this conversation to a close."

"Yeah, I think I'm going to take advantage of the quiet and sack out for a few minutes," responded Hogan as he lay down on the cot.

"Good idea!" replied Mike. And as his friend slept, Mike's mind came back to the present and to a traitor called 'Pretzel'.

Hogan's naps were shorter and less frequent than they had been the day before. As Schell had predicted, Hogan's strength was rapidly returning. With it, the old twinkle returned to his eyes. By the end of the day, he was getting down right restless and — bored! Hogan had taken to pacing the tunnel for as long as his weakened legs would allow him. Kinch barely caught him before he collapsed after he wandered into the radio room for what seemed like the five hundredth time that hour.

"Careful, sir, don't over do it," Kinch responded as he helped Hogan over to the cot.

"I'm not a child! You don't have to baby me!" Hogan protested sharply then, realizing he was letting his frustration control him, he softened his voice.

"Sorry I snapped," he replied remorsefully. "I appreciate the help, I really do. I'm just jumpy."

Kinch responded sympathetically, "It's ok, sir. After what you've been through, no one could blame you for being on edge."

"Kinch, do me a favor. Remind me the next time I design a tunnel to put in a window."

Kinch laughed, "I guess after three days it would seem a little close down here."

A little close! He hated to think about what Kinch considered a lot close. *It was stifling down here.* Hogan felt as though he were about to suffocate. He was dying to get upstairs to breathe fresh air again and to see sunshine. Hogan recalled how closed-in he felt during his first days at Stalag 13. He couldn't believe he had ever considered the camp confining. Of course, at the time he never dreamed he would spend a day having his mind held prisoner by his body and an additional two days stuck in a tunnel. The irony of the situation was the tunnel was of his own making. Hogan found himself a lot more sympathetic toward transient escapees forced to spend days in the tunnels before they could be transferred to the next station. Hogan made a mental note to expedite escapes more rapidly.

"What's happening in the outside world?" Hogan asked trying to get his mind off the narrowing walls of the tunnel.

"Not a whole lot. A little bit of sabotage here and there. London keeps calling to check on the status of 'Papa Bear'."

"Nice to know they care," Hogan replied sarcastically, then paused "Papa Bear?"

"Uh, yeah," stuttered Kinch. "That's the name Anders gave you when we where trying to get you away from the Gestapo and, well, it sort of stuck."

"Hummm, Papa Bear," mused Hogan. "You know, I like it!"

"We do too. Papa Bear just seems to fit better. No offense, sir, but you never really came across as the Goldilocks type."

"Then from here on out, Papa Bear it is," declared Hogan.

"One other thing, sir, London keeps asking for information about the German biological effort. They insist there is one in this area."

"What!?" ask Hogan angrily. He wasn't sure who was worse, Gottfried or London.

"Anders keeps putting them off by telling them he doesn't know anything, but he'll ask you," Kinch paused with a deadpan expression on his face, "When you come out of your coma."

"My what?"

"Your coma, sir, which, according to Dr. Schell relayed via Anders, won't be for at least a week."

Hogan chuckled. He'd have to remember that one. That was one way to get London off his back for a while. But London had to be warned about Pretzel before he led another agent into the hands of the Gestapo, one that might not be as lucky as he had been.

"Kinch, radio London, and tell them that Papa Bear has miraculously recovered from his 'coma' and has no information on a German bio effort. Tell them that Pretzel is a traitor and that the Gestapo will use him to gain access to an allied agent in order to obtain information on the allied bio program."

"London knows. The underground observed Pretzel leaving Gestapo headquarters the morning after the two of you were captured. We reported it as soon as we were informed."

"And…"

"Uh… well…" Kinch shuffled nervously, "That's when you went into a coma."

Apparently Anders and London had some differences of opinion over the whole Pretzel matter. The thought patterns (or lack there of) of the higher echelon never ceased to amaze him. *Smart move, the coma bit.* It gave them time to come up with a way to deal with Pretzel themselves. Hogan's mind began to work again.

CHAPTER 5
What Goes Around Comes Around

Gottfried had a habit of frequenting the local hofbraus at night and would be gone until the early hours of the morning. Lang waited patiently for Gottfried to leave. He had entered the villa, so far so good. The servants had the night off, so the villa was empty. It was the perfect time to carry out his plan. Lang walked down the hall toward the room which he knew to be Gottfried's study and entered the room before the study. It was filled with reels of movie film. Each canister had a number on it. On the desk was a notebook. Inside the notebook was a listing of the numbers on the film canisters, next to which was a date and a name. The films were obviously of interrogations, no wait! Some of these names Lang recognized. Some of these were ordinary citizens and some were Gottfried's own men, all loyal Germans. It unnerved him. The latest entry disturbed him even more. It was dated four days ago, next to it was written "cleaning lady." Gottfried had never even bothered to find out Greta's name. Lang took the reels out of the canisters, ripped the film off the reels and then left the room.

Next, Lang entered a room called the "Trophy Room." This room was filled with mannequins of people who were unfortunate enough to have met their demise at Gottfried's hands. Frightenly lifelike and proudly displayed in cases like trophies from a hunt, the mannequins were posed on medieval torture devices with expressions of agony forever frozen on their faces.

Lang made his way to the shop. There he found a meat locker, a bench, supplies for constructing mannequins, and the partially formed mannequin of a woman. On the table next to the mannequin was a list of numbers. Lang paled as he realized what they were and to whom they belonged. Walking over to the meat locker, Lang paused. He wasn't sure he really wanted to see its contents, but he had to. Taking a deep breath, Lang opened the door and went inside. Hanging from a hook like a slaughtered animal was Greta's body. Her sides were cut to shreds from stab wounds and her wrist and ankles were rubbed raw from her struggles against the shackles. Her face, that kind gentle face, had aged an eternity in the final moments of her life. Ernst Lang fought the urge to run. He had to stay, for there was work to be done if he was to give Greta's death meaning. Out of the corner of his eye, Ernst noticed a tarp and a gurney in the corner of the room. He took down Greta's body, wrapped it in the tarp, and laid it on the gurney.

"I will be back. I promise." Ernst said as he pulled the tarp up over her head. With that, Ernst closed the locker and left the room.

Sometime later Lang found his objective, Gottfried's "Playroom." He saw the table where Greta had died, still stained with her blood, and the raised platforms with movie cameras, which had recorded her tortured death. He saw racks in which persons literally had their limbs ripped from their bodies and other agonizing devices similar to the ones on which the mannequins were posed.

Lang returned to the shop and scattered everything he could find. He wheeled the gurney containing Greta's body into the playroom. Next, he tenderly placed the body back on the table on which she had died. Gingerly, he pulled the tarp away from her face.

"Forgive me, my friend, for letting you die such a horrible death. Forgive me for not being there for you, for bringing you back to this wretched place. You did not deserve to be tortured so. I'm so sorry, I'm so sorr..." Lang sobbed as he poured his heart out to his lifeless friend. "It should have been me. All you ever wanted was to be a friend, to help people. It was me who participated in the Gestapo's atrocities, and now you've paid the price. I promise, no one will ever die here again. I will see to it myself," Ernst vowed as he covered Greta's face for the last time with the tarp and doused her body with petrol.

With much of the country's petrol supply being needed for the war effort, very little was available for civilian use. What was available came with a very high price tag, but Ernst had managed to obtain some. Ernst had to destroy Gottfried's playroom, but he couldn't bear the thought of leaving his friend's body to be further mutilated by that pervert, of having her become one of his trophies, but he didn't have enough petrol to burn both the playroom and the shop. While the shop probably contained enough flammable material to destroy the room completely and everything in it once lit, still he couldn't take the chance that somehow Greta's body would not be incinerated. That would be a more hideous crime than what had already been done to her. The only way he could guarantee both would be destroyed was to bring Greta's body back to the playroom and burn it with the room. He hoped that in some small manner his act would provide Greta the dignity, and the respect as a human being that had been stripped from her in life. Then she could rest in peace.

When he finished dousing the body, Lang doused the cameras, and everything else he could, lit a match, and ran.

The room went up like a torch. On the way out, Ernst threw a couple matches into the ransacked shop, trophy room, and film storage areas. For some unexplainable reason, prior to throwing a match into Gottfried's study, Ernst paused long enough to notice and remove a notebook. He wasn't sure why, but for some reason he felt it might be important. Without a doubt, Ernst had fated himself to become the subject of one of Gottfried's perverted interrogations, for he deserved no less. But if in doing so, he could prevent one innocent person from suffering the same fate, his death — and more importantly, Greta's — would not be in vain.

* * *

If only Bonnie could see me now, mused Tiptoe as he prepared to meet another day as Colonel Hogan. Now that the colonel was well on his way to recovery, Tiptoe had been become insufferable in his newly found position of power. *Too bad I've only got four more days. Maybe I'll have a picture made and send it to Bonnie.*

Bonnie Easterday was a dynamite brunette back home with a shapely hourglass figure and beautiful brown eyes like melted chocolate. Kind, sweet, sensitive with never a bad word about anybody and a great sense of humor, Bonnie could almost outwit him — almost! Boy, could she play a mean piano. Bonnie could play anything from "Amazing Grace" to Mozart and she loved music as much as he did.

But that wasn't the best thing about Bonnie, oh no, the best thing about Bonnie was her cooking. She made the best biscuits and gravy Tiptoe had ever put in his mouth and he loved biscuits and gravy. The one thing Tiptoe absolutely hated about Germany was — no biscuits and gravy. Even LeBeau, who was rumored to be the best cook in captivity, didn't have a clue as to how to make biscuits and gravy. It boggled the mind as to how a great French chef couldn't cook a simple little thing like biscuits and gravy. How hard could it be? After all, the French put sauces on everything. Why couldn't they make biscuits and gravy? Maybe he could get Bonnie to send him the recipe, and then if he asked nicely LeBeau would cook it for him. The thought of having to talk nicely to someone made Tiptoe cringe. It was more fun to give orders. Tiptoe sighed, being a private again was going to be tough. Oh well... Tiptoe's mind wandered back to Bonnie. Yeah, Bonnie was a wonderful girl all right. She deserved the very best. Tiptoe only hoped she didn't go off and do something stupid like get married before he had a chance to come home and show her just what the best really was.

Over the past four days, it had become a habit for the men of Barracks 12 to stall during roll call until Tiptoe came sliding in at the last minute after completing roll call in Barracks 2. Because Roth believed Tiptoe to be Hogan, everybody just expected it to continue until Klink returned. It came as a total surprise when Tiptoe came strolling up to roll call — on time!

Private Ron Williams leaned over and whispered to Tiptoe as they were lining up, "Hey, Tippy! You're early, what's the matter? The colonel bust you back to private?"

"Not yet," replied Hogan smugly in the private's uniform. "But give it about four days."

It was an amusing sight watching Williams stutter and stammer once he realized it was Hogan in Tiptoe's uniform. Hogan never thought they looked that much alike.

Just goes to show you how much people really pay attention to the man inside the uniform.

Hogan fought to suppress a grin as whispers passed down

the line and men suddenly were on their best behavior once they realized Hogan was in the line up. It was a cold winter's day, but Hogan didn't really feel it. He basked in the sunlight. It was great to be above ground to see the sky and to feel the breeze on his cheek. Hogan felt wonderful. It was great to be alive.

Christmas was a little over a week away. Now that life was almost back to normal, if indeed life in Stalag 13 was ever truly normal, rehearsals for the "Living Christmas Tree" were hot and heavy. The choir had just finished rehearsing a particularly difficult piece when Tiptoe addressed them.

"That brought tears to my eyes," he said sweetly. Then his demeanor abruptly turned harsh and demanding as he added, "Don't ever let me hear it again!"

Mockingly Tiptoe began to lecture, "Now men, look at your music. A dark rectangle, a squiggle, and no that's not a medical insignia, one of those things that looks like a spear with a feather on it, or a spear with two feathers on it. Each of those things is called a 'rest'. A rest means *don't* sing."

He continued, "The little round balls, the little round balls with sticks on them, the dark little round balls with sticks on them, and the dark little round balls with sticks and flags on them, those are called 'notes'. A note means *do* sing. Now do we all understand that? Are there any questions?"

"Ah, excuse me," came a timid voice from the back. "What are the squashed looking balls with stems on them?"

"Those are called flats. And that's what your head is going to be if I hear you singing during a rest again!" admonished Tiptoe with mock anger. His comment was drawing giggles and snickers from the choir.

"You see these," he said pointing to the eagles on the shoulders of Hogan's jacket, seeing Hogan standing in the background as he turned. Hogan had slipped in unobserved to check on the choir's progress. Without missing a beat, Tiptoe continued, "They belong to him," pointing to Hogan, "and HE doesn't want to hear those sounds either."

Hogan choked back a laugh, gave Tiptoe the sternest look he could muster given the circumstances, and replied in a tone of command, "Just make sure you remember who those eagles belong to, PRIVATE!!!"

Turning, Hogan exited as hastily as he could while pretending to stroll casually. After all, he had to maintain some degree of dignity. He was an officer. It was his job to maintain discipline. Plus, he had a reputation to maintain. Only when he was outside did Hogan allow himself to react fully to Tiptoe's remarks. Hogan laughed until his ribs hurt. It was a good feeling. Hogan really couldn't blame Tiptoe for coming down on the choir. As a young officer Hogan had played drums for a swing band. The importance of timing both from a musical and mission perspective was not lost on Hogan, and the timing on that piece was pretty bad!

* * *

Lang had done his work well. Between the petroleum, the chemicals, and other flammable materials, Gottfried's villa was a flaming inferno before anyone could get near it. The heat from the flames was so intense nothing could have been done to save the villa (short of having advanced knowledge of Lang's plan and stopping him), not that anybody in the town was too upset at seeing Gottfried's castle-of-evil burn. But the town's sense of relief was short lived, all too soon replaced by terror. Gottfried was outraged upon his return to the smoking embers of his home.

"Heads will roll!" he proclaimed.

And roll they did. Gottfried's first action was to shoot the fire marshal. After all, it was the fire marshal's job to prevent and extinguish fires. If his villa could burn to the ground, obviously the fire marshal was inept. Upon discovering evidence of arson, Gottfried turned his attention to his own organization. He found the officer on duty at the time of the burning and shot him. The man was obviously incapable of ferreting out and crushing defiance of authority; therefore, he was incompetent and not deserving to live. Gottfried took the attack personally, turning into a violent lunatic, extracting vengeance on anybody he could find to blame.

Gottfried began rounding up people from town. Somebody had information and he would find out who. Until then, everybody was a suspect. Long sturdy metal rods were installed in rooms with high ceilings at Gestapo headquarters. Large groups of suspects where hung from these rods by chains thrown over the rods and shackled to their wrists. They hung suspended by their arms, their feet bound with balls and chains. Without support from the feet, the weight of the suspects' bodies and confines pulled painfully on their arms, threatening to wretch them from their sockets. Suspects were stacked along the length of the pipe like clothes in an overstuffed closet.

"Tell me who did this!" Gottfried demanded.

The suspects remained silent, terrified of the raging madman and what he would do.

Infuriated, Gottfried forcefully cracked a whip down the line, across the side of each person. Screams of pain filled the room.

"Please, sir, I am a harmless old man, I know nothing of value. Please sir, let me go," pleaded an elderly man.

"I will determine what is of value and what isn't. Now talk!

Nobody leaves here until I find out who set my villa on fire. Somebody knows something. Talk! Talk! Or everybody dies!" ordered Gottfried, the flames from the villa now resurrected in his eyes as he mercilessly beat the prisoners again and again.

Between the beatings and hangings, most of the suspects moaned in pain, death preferable to torture, and many swore their ignorance and begged for release. The pleading and screams, which normally would have delighted Gottfried, only made him angrier. The angrier he became the more viciously he beat the captives. Right now the only pleasure left in Gottfried's world was the thought of what he would do when he found the man who destroyed his trophies and his research. Gottfried's one obsession in life was finding the man who destroyed his world.

* * *

Since London refused to acknowledge the fact that Pretzel was a double agent, Hogan and Anders were meeting in Hogan's office to devise a plan for dealing with Pretzel.

"Whatever we do, it's going to be tricky," Anders stated.

"Yeah," agreed Hogan, contemplating the situation. "If we set up a meeting, he's going to have a ton of Gestapo with him. There must have been at least two squads when I was grabbed. Gottfried will have that much, if not more. Since he lost his first golden goose, he's not going to take chances with a second." Even now, the thoughts of another encounter with Gottfried sent chills down Hogan's spine. There had to be a way of drawing Pretzel out alone.

A knock on the door interrupted their conversation. Kinch entered handing Hogan a piece of paper. Hogan frowned as he read the message.

"Sorry to interrupt you, but I just got this message from Moonglow."

"What is it?" asked Anders.

"The underground unit in Cologne has disbanded. It appears Gottfried is pursuing them. Prior to that, they managed to pass along some information Felix thinks is pretty important. He would like to arrange a meeting for tonight." Hogan replied.

"Kinch, radio Felix back and tell him to meet me tonight at 2200, the usual place. Have Newkirk meet him and bring him into camp."

"Right, Colonel."

Hogan paced the room. Then he paused in thought and crossed his arms.

"What's wrong?" ask Anders as Kinch left the office.

"I don't know, I can't put my finger on it, but something *feels* wrong. Why all this sudden interest in underground activity now? Considering Gottfried's previous obsession with getting his hands on information concerning the allied biological defense program, I'd think he would be laying plans on how to grab another allied agent. It doesn't make sense."

"Maybe he's trying to divert suspicion from his real objective. Get us to drop our guard on the bio issue," suggested Anders.

"Could be. On the other hand, I seemed to remember Gottfried mentioning a fire at a fuel depot. If it was a total loss, I can't see that sitting very well with his superiors. It could be Gottfried's trying to save face in Berlin while he comes up with another plan for gaining access to information on the allied bio programs." Hogan let out a sigh, "I don't know. Let's see what Felix has to say."

* * *

Lang knew better than to hang around and admire his handy work. He had left town the second he lit the last match in Gottfried's villa. For the moment he was safe, but not for long. The instant Gottfried realized Lang had fled Cologne, he would know exactly where to find him. Any chance at all to escape Greta's fate lay in his ability to flee the country.

What made him take the notebook from Gottfried's study he didn't know, but since he had it, Lang decided to take a look. As he read the contents, Lang turned pasty white. Inside were detailed plans for an offensive biological program. The nightmares he had feared were all there and worse. Germany was the aggressor, the allies the target. Defensive biological warfare was a reasonable pursuit. The objective of a defensive biological program, such as vaccine development, was not to cause suffering but to prevent suffering. Offensive biological warfare was quite another story. It was a blatant disregard for human life, an abomination against God and man. For the first time in his life Lang was ashamed to be German. He had to warn the allies. If he died trying, so be it.

* * *

Newkirk met Felix at the rendezvous point and brought him into camp. Felix looked at Anders suspiciously.

"He's all right," Hogan assured Felix. "I can vouch for him. What do you have for us?"

"Last night after midnight," Felix began, "We got a call from Nighthawk. It seems someone burned Gottfried's private villa. In retaliation Gottfried began a reign of terror, which included gathering towns people for interrogation. Nighthawk was afraid Gottfried would learn about their operation, so they disbanded and fled the city."

"Any of them here?" Hogan asked, wondering how

different Gottfried's reign of terror was over his usual reign and deciding he really didn't want to know.

"No, they used other escape routes."

"Good," replied Hogan.

With Pretzel on the loose and Gottfried on the prowl, the last thing Hogan needed was a visit from Hochsetter and his band of merry men.

"You said Gottfried's private villa was burned? Why would anyone be interested in Gottfried's residence?" asked Anders. This time it was Anders with the feeling of something gone awry.

"I don't know. Nighthawk didn't say. But it must have some significance or Gottfried wouldn't be on such a vendetta."

"Since when does the Gestapo need a good reason to go on a vendetta?" grumbled Newkirk.

"There is something else," Felix continued, ignoring Newkirk's remark, "Pretzel was in town today."

"By town, do you mean Düsseldorf?" a puzzled Anders inquired. Why would Pretzel be in Düsseldorf? This made no sense at all.

"Yes, Düsseldorf."

"How do you know it was Pretzel?"

"Several days ago, when Nighthawk reported a man fitting the description of Goldilocks had been captured, I went down to Cologne to confirm the identity of the prisoner. In the process, I also saw the man captured with him, the one assumed to be his contact, Pretzel. It was that man I saw in Düsseldorf."

"Did he recognize you?" This time the question came from Hogan.

"No, I saw *him* in Cologne, but he never saw *me*. He has no reason to think I'm anything but a man on the street."

Hogan and Anders looked at each other with that *Are you thinking what I'm thinking?* look. Then Hogan smiled that impish grin, which always meant he was up to something.

"What have you got cooking, sir?" asked a jubilant LeBeau expectantly. He was nearly jumping up and down with excitement.

"I'm thinking maybe we can use this to our advantage and we can lead Pretzel into our trap," answered Hogan. "Felix, you think you can find him again, slip him a note or something inconspicuous so that he doesn't see you and arrange a meeting for tomorrow night at, oh, say, 2200."

"That should not be a problem. He's been all over town trying to make contact with the underground. He told Karl at the hofbrau he has important information on the German biological program that he wants to pass to the allies. When he left town we followed him to the old abandoned farmhouse on the Cologne road. It seems to be his base."

"Did he meet anybody?" Hogan inquired.

"No. Other than his attempts to contact the underground, he saw or spoke to no one, and he didn't meet any one at the farmhouse."

"Good work. Set a meeting for 2200 at the farmhouse. We'll handle it from there. Keep your distance from him. Make indirect contact only, use notes or whatever. Don't let him see you, and tell Karl to lay low for a while. If Pretzel is setting up a trap, I don't want any of your men getting caught in it."

Felix nodded.

I believe this is where I came in, thought Anders.

Hogan too had a strange feeling of déjà vu. Pretzel wasn't wasting any time looking for his next pigeon. *With Gottfried right on his tail,* mused Hogan. Apparently the fire *was* a diversion to throw them off guard. Well, that street ran two ways.

"You've been a big help. Thanks. LeBeau, see him out the tunnel."

"Oui, colonel."

As LeBeau and Felix left the tunnel, the rest of Hogan's men gathered around.

"You're not really planning to meet that guy again are you, sir?" inquired Kinch.

"Of course, I am. I never break a date!" *Unless she's a dog.*

"Carter, run and fetch Schell; I think the Colonel is having a relapse. Why don't you just sit down over here and relax, sir. A couple days rest and you'll be a new man."

Hogan responded to Newkirk's chides with a look of distain and Anders stifled a chuckle.

"Colonel, you can't go," Newkirk said. "You just said yourself it's probably a Gestapo trap. It'll be like a ruddy SS convention."

"No it won't. We're going to give the Gestapo another party to go to." Hogan retorted as his men looked at each other in mass confusion.

* * *

Gottfried's unstable frame of mind created an atmosphere of sheer terror in Gestapo headquarters. He shot people for no better reason than he didn't like their height, weight, tone of voice, or hairstyle. Gotffried's personal staff even went out of their way to avoid him. Chaos reigned as the officers in charge scrambled to decide who was going to report the results of the latest investigation to the colonel. Taking advantage of their ranks, the officers delegated the responsibility down until it reached the lowest level of enlisted men. There, the men cast lots to determine who would be the one to take fate in his hands by being the messenger.

Private Mueller lost the draw. He stood nervously in front of Gottfried's door, trying to regain his composure before he went in.

"Colonel, sir," Mueller addressed his commanding officer as he walked in, clicked his heels, and stood at attention.

Gottfried scowled, fire still blazing in his eyes, at the young private,. "What is it?" he barked.

"Sir, this was found in the woods near the villa, sir," the private replied handing Gottfried a locket, then returning to stand at attention. "It is believed to have belonged to the saboteur, sir. The pictures in the locket, sir, are of Johann and Luisa Lang. They lived on a farm near Düsseldorf until 1928 when they left to live with Lusia's sister in Berlin. Johann died in 1930. Luisa died in 1935. They had one son, Ernst. Ernst lives in Cologne. He is a Gestapo collaborator."

Gottfired smiled for the first time since the fire.

"Was a Gestapo collaborator. Now he is a traitor. Very good, tell Captain Schmitt to be in the woods near the old Lang farm tonight at 2100 with two squads of men. Tell him to have them hide in the woods out of sight until I tell them to move in."

He'd teach Lang a lesson. A lesson he'd never forget.

"What's your name?"

"Private Henrik Mueller, sir," said Mueller standing straight at attention.

"Private Mueller, good work. I want you at the farm tonight. Who knows," said Gottfried the wicked gleam competing with the glowing fire in his eyes, as he rose and made his way to the door, "If your performance is satisfactory, there maybe something in this for you."

"Danke, sir," replied Mueller saluting as Gottfried walked out the door.

All of Cologne breathed a great sigh of relief as Gottfried left on his hunt for Lang. With the saboteur identified and Gottfried's psychopathic obsession focused on him, they were safe. Safe, that is, until his obsession unpredictably changed its focus yet again.

Upon leaving Gestapo headquarters Gottfried commandeered a civilian car, returned to his rented hotel room, and changed into civilian clothes. He put a pair of handcuffs and leg irons in a pack and headed toward Düsseldorf. It had been a long time since he had personally done undercover work. When one was a colonel, one had others do the dirty work. This time it was personal, and Gottfried would trust no one but himself. Gottfried was an accomplished spy. Spying was like riding a bike: once the skill was acquired, it was never lost.

Gottfried knew exactly where to find Lang: at the homestead.

Lang, that little mealy-mouthed ingrate!

The thought made Gottfried's blood boil. Gottfried was omnipotent. Nobody, but nobody defied Gottfried. The ones who even tried quickly found out the full extent of Gottfried's power and wrath. Lang was a sentimental fool. Gottfried knew it because he had been able to use that sentimentality for his own purposes. Gottfried poisoned his mind against the allies, convincing him that all the bad things that had happened to him in the world had been the fault of the allies. The failure of the farm and the premature deaths of his parents were all because of the economic collapse of Germany, all the fault of the allies. And he had believed it and had led an important allied agent right into his hands. The agent would have given

Gottfried all the secrets of the allied biological program had that idiot, Ritter, not killed him with his drugs. Someday Ritter, too, would pay. Having Lang meet the agent in the old homestead, the place where he grew up, had been sheer genius. Surrounded by visual reminders of his parents' failure reinforced his conviction of the allies' guilt, which only heightened his allegiance to Gottfried's cause. And now sentiment would be his undoing. Gottfried knew sooner or later that Lang *would* return to the homestead. All Gottfried had to do was wait.

* * *

Schmitt was assigning a detail of men to meet Gottfried when the phone rang.

"Gestapo headquarters. Heil Hitler!"

"This is General Kinchhoff from Reichsfuhrer Himmler's personal staff. I want to speak to Colonel Gottfried."

Oh no, not again, thought Schmitt.

"Colonel Gottfried is not here, I am Captain Schmitt, may I help you, sir?"

"Colonel Gottfried is not there! Where is he? I must speak to him, get him right away!"

"Sir, the colonel is undercover. I have no way of contacting him," explained a very nervous Schmitt.

"In that case, listen and listen closely: Reichsführer Himmler is secretly on an inspection tour in search of a new second-in-command to replace Heyrdrich.[21] He will be arriving in Cologne tonight. The reichsführer must be protected at all cost! I want every man you have to be at the train station at 2200. No one is to leave the station for any reason without either the reichsführer's order or mine. No one! Do you understand?"

"Yes, sir, all available personnel will be at the train station at 2200."

"Dummkopf, I said *every* man, not *all available* men. Do you know the meaning of the word 'every'?"

"But sir, the colonel has ordered two squads of men to his area tonight. He expects those men to be there to arrest some dangerous underground agents. Otherwise, the saboteurs may escape. The colonel himself may even be injured or killed."

"Dummkopf, how did you get to be a captain? The same assassins who killed Heydrich may try to kill Himmler. The safety of the reichsführer is of the utmost importance, much more important than a petty little band of saboteurs or even a colonel. I want every man at the station, *every* man — no exceptions! Do I make myself clear?"

"Jawohl, herr general, it shall be done. I will see to it personally. Heil Hitler!" Gottfried could only kill him once. Schmitt was tired of living in fear. At this point, he would just as soon Gottfried shot him and be done with it.

"It had better be, or heads will roll! Heil Hitler!" barked Kinchhoff (otherwise known as Stalag 13 radioman Ivan Kinchloe).

Hogan hovered anxiously over Kinch as he broke off the connection.

"Gottfried wasn't there, so I talked to a Captain Schmitt..."

"Hey," interrupted Carter excitedly, "Wasn't that the guy we talked to when we tried to break the colonel out of jail?"

"Now that you mention it, that name does sound familiar," mused Newkirk.

"Didn't you go in as a General from Himmler's personal staff? What name did you use?" asked Anders.

"General Franz. Why?" inquired Newkirk.

"Two different people claiming to be generals from

Himmler's personal staff with two different names might make Schmitt suspicious."

"I don't think so," Newkirk responded. "We identified ourselves only to the corporal on duty. He called Schmitt. Since we never gave our names to this Schmitt fellow, the different names wouldn't give it away. As far as the voices go, over the phone I doubt he could tell that Kinch wasn't Carter.

"What about it Kinch? Did he sound like he was on to you?" asked Hogan.

"No, as I was saying," Kinch continued, "this Schmitt was a little reluctant at first, but he didn't sound like he thought anything was up."

"You said he was reluctant, why?" asked Hogan.

"Schmitt said Gottfried was away, undercover. He claimed Gottfried was trying to find some dangerous underground agents. Gottfried expects to make arrests tonight. Gottfried had ordered two squads to meet him. Schmitt was hesitant to commit them to the train station out of fear of the consequences to that mission."

"If that's true, then Pretzel really is laying a trap."

"It looks that way, sir," agreed Kinch.

"What about the two squads?"

"I made it pretty clear I wanted everybody at the station. Schmitt did say he would see to it personally."

"Colonel, you are not planning on going through with this, are you?" LeBeau asked with concern.

"I am. *If* the patrols are pulled away, we will out number him. The odds will be in our favor."

"But what if Schmitt is suspicious. What if he doesn't pull the patrols?" Kinch questioned.

"We'll set up our own patrol in the woods. He can't put that many men in the woods without us knowing it. The minute we see any signs of troop movement, we scrub the mission."

Anders had been deep in thought. Something still didn't seem right but he didn't know what.

"Colonel, could I talk to you please."

"Ok, guys that's all for now."

Picking up on Anders' hint, Hogan's men scattered above ground.

"Ok, Mike what is it?"

"What if Pretzel doesn't show up? Have you thought about that? Suppose Schmitt *did* buy Kinch's story and as a result, *they* scrub *their* mission. What if Pretzel returns and nobody shows up? What then?"

"Then we start over."

The possibility of Pretzel not showing was something Hogan had not even considered. A no-show on Pretzel's part would put them right back at square one. Hogan hated it when people got realistic on him while he was on a roll.

"We know Pretzel is out in the field, so he is pretty much inaccessible until he reports in. I suspect life at Gestapo headquarters is pretty chaotic now, so odds are he won't get word to abort the mission."

"In which case, there *still* may be patrols in the woods. Any way you look at it the odds are good that if we encounter Pretzel, we encounter patrols." Anders went on to add, "I don't think you should go."

"Mike, if we don't get this guy, he's going to lead someone else into the Gestapo's trap. It's obvious he's setting a trap right now. You know that as well as I do, and London's not going to listen until it's too late. It's just a matter of time before he catches a fish. And this fish may end up giving the Krauts the information they want. It's up to us to catch this guy ourselves, *now,* before that happens. This is our best chance. Maybe our only chance."

"I know and I agree; however, I think I should be the one to meet Pretzel."

As Hogan opened his mouth to respond, Mike continued, not giving Hogan a chance to argue.

"Look Robert, four days ago you were at death's door and you still have residual weakness from the poison whether you want to admit it or not. It's too soon for you to be going out on a mission like this. Give it some more time. I can handle this. After all, I am a trained spy."

"I'm fine, Mike and I'm going." Hogan declared in voice of command that allowed for no dissention.

"Ok, have it your way," Mike conceded, knowing that once Hogan made up his mind, it was pointless to argue with him. "But do me a favor, as a friend at least let me go with you."

This time it was Hogan's turn to concede. After all, Mike had been the first to see Pretzel for the traitor that he was. Hogan owed it to Mike to let him in on the capture.

* * *

The old Lang homestead was covered by so much growth it had been easy to sneak up on an unsuspecting Goldilocks and capture him. Although a great deal of the bush had been pulled up and disturbed during the capture and arrest of the allied agent, there was sufficient foliage left to cover the movement of one man. Gottfried moved in and checked out the house and barn. No one was there. *Not yet!* Lang would be there. Of this Gottfried was certain. And when he came, Gottfried would be waiting. Near the house Gottfried dug a hole in the ground where he could see both the house and the barn. Then he buried himself, pulling bush over the mound. He blended with the landscape so well no one, including Lang, would notice him until it was too late. Gottfried would have him!

Gottfried waited. While he waited, he entertained himself with the thought of what he would do to Lang once he caught him. He would handcuff him to a tree and let him watch while he burned to the ground what was left of his beloved home. *An eye for an eye, or rather, a villa for a farm,* Gottfried mused. Better yet, he would let Lang watch from inside the blazing structure, bound hand and foot unable to escape the flames. The sounds of his tortured screams as he burned, like the soothing sounds of a symphony. Dusk fell, still no Lang. Where could he be?

Anders, Hogan, and Hogan's men moved out at 2100. They combed the grounds and woods around the farmhouse and the barn. The Moonglow unit stationed itself at the crossroad from Cologne to Düsseldorf ready to report back any signs of troop movement. Hogan's men continued to patrol the parameter of the homestead. At 2145 all stations reported "clear."

"Looks, like this Schmitt fella took Kinch seriously. *So far, so good.* I'll take the farmhouse, you take the barn." Hogan ordered Anders. Hogan and Anders moved cautiously to their perspective assignments.

In the darkness, dressed in camouflage, and because of the distance the barn was from the house, Gottfried could not see Anders move into the barn nor had he seen the men comb the grounds. Against the backdrop of the moon, he did catch a glimpse of Hogan's silhouette as he entered the farmhouse. *Now I have him!* Gottfried grabbed his pack, jumped from his hiding place, and rushed into the house.

"Halt, put down the gun!" he ordered as Hogan turned to face him, gun drawn. Hogan froze as he found himself staring down the barrel of Gottfried's Luger. "Over there, by the window, where I can see you. Schnell! Schnell!"

Hogan slowly and carefully put the gun down, and then just as slowly moved toward the window. He had to find a way to warn Anders and his men without Gottfried realizing they were around. Watching Hogan like a hawk, Gottfried yelled for his men in the woods to advance and take the prisoner.

Well, if that doesn't tell guys something is wrong, nothing will.

Now he needed to buy time for his men and Anders to act.

"So, you think you can burn my villa and get away with it. You fool! I'll show you what happens to fools."

Where was Schmitt? Where were his men? Was he surrounded by fools? Never mind, he didn't need them, he could do this himself. Gottfried retrieved the handcuffs from his pack, not taking his eyes or his gun off Hogan.

"Hold out your hands," he ordered.

As Hogan moved into the light shining through the window, Gottfried recognized him.

"*You!* You're not Lang, you're Goldilocks and you're not dead! You tricked me!" Gottfried screamed, rage blazing in his eyes, "This time I will see to it that your death is permanent!"

With that, Gotffried dropped the handcuffs and pulled the trigger. Hogan saw a muzzle flash and simultaneously felt himself body-tackled, then darkness.

Gottfried wasn't the only one hiding; Lang too had been hiding. Alarmed by the dangers of meeting at the farmhouse but unable to warn the underground, he had hidden in the one place he knew Gottfried would not look, under the back porch. The porch hardly looked like the kind of place a person could hide. It was low to the ground and boarded all the way around except for a small opening hidden behind a bush next to the house. If one didn't know it was there, one would never suspect it. Lang knew about it because he had hidden there many times as a child. In horror, Lang had seen Gottfried search the back of the house and knew he would be close by, watching, waiting. Lang knew his underground contact was a dead man, but he didn't know what to do, so he stayed hidden. At the sound of commotion inside the house, Lang realized the contact had arrived and Gottfried had him. He had to do something. He couldn't let another man die because of him. Cautiously, Lang crawled out of his hiding place and sneaked in the back way. Inside the house, he saw Gottfried with his gun aimed at the contact. Lang lunged. The last sound he heard was Gottfried's gun firing.

Anders had completed his inspection of the barn and was halfway to the house when he heard Gottfried's shouts. He ran the rest of the way and arrived in time to see Gottfried fire.

"Halt!" Anders shouted.

A stark raving mad Gottfried turned to face Anders, his gun raised. Without thinking twice Anders fired, hitting Gottfried squarely in the chest. Gottfried staggered and raised his gun again. Anders fired twice more, hitting Gottfried again squarely in the chest. This time Gottfried fell and did not move. Anders kicked the gun away from Gottfried's body. Carefully, he checked the pulse. It was over. Gottfried was dead.

Two motionless figures lay in a pile. Mike now turned his attention to them.

"Robert? Robert!" Mike shouted in alarm.

Silence. Gottfried only fired one shot. How could he have he hit both of them? Who was this other person?

Hogan was on the bottom of the pile. As Mike gently

rolled the body of the unidentified man off Hogan, Hogan began to stir. Hogan's men came running through both entrances of the house weapons drawn. Their first sight was the body in the doorway. As Kinch checked Gottfried's pulse, Carter sighted the semi-conscious form of his commanding officer and screamed.

"Colonel Hogan!"

"He'll be alright. He just got the wind knocked out of him that's all," Anders reassured the shocked sergeant.

Stubborn mule, I knew I should have hog-tied him and left him behind. The other man was a different story: the side of his face was covered in blood, but he was still breathing.

"Carter, Kinch, lookout. Newkirk, see what you can do for this fella," ordered Anders as he moved to help his friend.

With the residual effects of the poison and having been smashed between the floor and his rescuer, Hogan was having problems breathing. Mike carefully lifted Hogan's upper body and supported him in a sitting position so he could breathe better.

"Who hit me?" a dazed Hogan gasped.

"That guy over there," Mike responded motioning to Lang's unconscious form.

"Dead?"

"No, the bullet just grazed him, but he's going to have one bloody awful headache when he wakes up," Newkirk replied, cleaning and bandaging the wound as best he could with his handkerchief. "He is a lucky man."

"Do you have any idea who he is?" Mike asked Hogan.

With Anders help, Hogan slowly and carefully moved so he could get a good look at the man. His ribs ached and were probably bruised.

"Don't kid with me. I don't feel like it. You know as well as I do, he's Pretzel."

"Now I don't get it. First he turns me in, then he saves my life."

Mike scowled, "That's not Pretzel. Pretzel's dead. Are you sure you're all right? Maybe I should get Dr. Schell to take a look at you when we get back."

Hogan didn't respond.

"He's Pretzel, he's not Pretzel. The whole thing is making me dizzy," commented LeBeau.

Hogan looked at the man he had thought of as Pretzel, the man just starting to come to, and then he looked at Gottfried's body. "Of course! This guy was a decoy. Gottfried was really Pretzel. How could I have missed it?"

Hogan admonished Anders, "If you knew Gottfried was Pretzel, why didn't you tell me?"

"I assumed he was the man who met you and, therefore, you knew. I recognized him from the picture in his file. Which… which I saw in London and you *never* saw," Mike replied slowly, as the realization dawned on him that Hogan never had a way of knowing what the real Pretzel looked like.

"Opps!" Mike responded, hand over his mouth and eyes rolled up like a kid with his hand caught in the candy jar.

"Opps, is right!" agreed Hogan glaring his disapproval at Mike while making a mental note to do his homework more thoroughly before a mission. Their attention was diverted back to a moaning Lang.

"Ohhhh! My head hurts!"

"Take it easy, mate. You are going to be all right," said Newark.

Lang looked at Newkirk, trying to focus his vision. Finally he said, "You are British."

"Please, don't tell me mum. It would break her heart. She thinks I'm Welsh."

"Then you must be with the underground."

"He works for me," Hogan said entering the conversation.

Lang stared at Hogan, "No, it can't be. You are dead."

"Not quite, Goldilocks is dead," Hogan corrected, giving Anders a dirty look, which he ignored, "but I am very much alive. I'm Papa Bear."

"Papa Bear, my contact?" Lang moaned in pain.

"Yes," Hogan replied sympathetically. He still wasn't feeling great himself.

"Gottfried plans to start an extensive offensive biological research program." Hogan and Anders looked at each other with puzzled looks. "Under the back porch is a notebook. It contains detailed plans."

"Ok, take it easy, we'll get it," Hogan replied.

Newkirk helped Lang to sit while LeBeau went to retrieve the book. LeBeau searched for an opening to crawl into and found none.

"He did say under the porch?" LeBeau yelled into the house.

"Oh, I forgot to tell you, there's a small opening behind the bush. It's the only way in."

"Look behind the bush!" Newkirk yelled back.

LeBeau looked again. Hidden behind the bush he found a small space barely big enough to crawl into. *You've got to be kidding! A dog couldn't get in here much less a man!* LeBeau wiggled in, got the book, and wiggled back out uttering a few choice French words along the way.

"Gottfried's dead, so I don't think he's going to be starting any bio efforts. But, we are going to get that book and you to

London," Hogan informed Lang as LeBeau returned with the book. "It's a hike back to base, think you're up to it?"

"Yes, I think so," Lang replied.

"Good," said Hogan as he picked up his radio. "Papa Bear calling Moonglow. Mission accomplished. Return to base. Repeat, return to base. Papa Bear, out." Hogan and his group returned to their base as well with Lang in tow.

Thinking his services were no longer needed, Schell had originally planned to return to Berlin that night. However, the plans Hogan and Anders had made to capture Pretzel sounded dangerous enough that Schell decided he had better postpone his trip another day "just in case."

While Schell treated Lang's injuries, Hogan and Anders examined Gottfried's lab book in the privacy of Hogan's office.

"Labs, crematoriums, barracks, arms magazines, farms, autopsy facilities, dissection facilities, holding cells. This looks like a plan for a complete biological experimentation facility," commented Anders.

"Take a look at this," Hogan read, "Anthrax, plague, typhoid, smallpox, frostbite, the list goes on and on. Gottfried planned to look at every known thing under the sun. Look at the experiments he planned to perform. Not just on animals, but *humans* as well. 'Dissect healthy subjects to establish a baseline, inject subjects with pathogen, observe reaction of subjects to pathogen, tie healthy subjects to stakes given distances from a pathogen release point, release pathogens, study proximity affect of pathogens on the subjects, dissect subjects.' Sometimes he's dissecting them while they are still alive. All right outside Cologne in our backyard. This is disgusting! Here, see for yourself."

Hogan passed the book to Anders.

Anders read the book in silence, not believing what he was seeing. He was so sure Hitler and, thus, Germany were anti-offensive bio. With his own ears he had heard the proclamations, yet here, undeniably, in black and white were detailed plans for a very elaborate, very thorough offensive bio program. Gottfried very clearly had been insane even for a Gestapo officer. But, was this the work of a deranged officer, or was it possible Himmler on his own initiative had decided to launch an offensive bio program? It all ran counter to the facts. Anders pondered the question briefly. He read on, then paused.

"I think you'd better take a look at this," he said quietly.

Hogan took the book and read the passage Anders pointed out to him. He turned pale.

"Gottfried planned to use Staglag 13 as a source for human subjects!"

Numb, Hogan put the book down on his desk, walked over to the window, cracked the shutters, and stared. He stared at the rows of barracks. He thought about the men sleeping inside, the ones who depended on him to keep them safe. The thoughts of those same men as the objects of Gottfried's perverse experiments made him physically ill. Suddenly the camp became smaller, more stifling than ever before.

Air, he needed air. Even in death Gottfried haunted him, choking him. Hogan wanted to run across the barracks, down the tunnel, out the emergency tunnel, and take the escape route back to England where he could breathe again, where he could be free from Gotffried and his terrors. But not free from the men who trusted him, depended on him, not free from himself! Hogan's mind was drawn back to that brief moment in time shortly after his poisoning, when Hogan was so sure he was dying. Hogan remembered his regrets at not having adequately provided for his men. It seemed Hogan was being given a second chance, and he was not a man to make the same mistake twice. When he spoke, Hogan's voice bore the full weight of the responsibility he shouldered, strong and determined.

"I need to come up with an evacuation plan," Hogan announced still staring out the window.

Anders nodded in acknowledgment of Hogan's responsibility to the men in his charge. Mike had always worked alone. He couldn't image what it was like to be responsibile for other men's lives on a daily basis. He didn't envy his friend that responsibility. As Hogan, deep in thought, continued staring out the window, Mike walked over and put his hand on his friend's shoulder.

"Robert," he said softly. "Do what you must. An evacuation plan is an excellent idea. But before you make your final decision, let me give you the benefit of my intelligence and observation in this arena.

"Hitler has been very adamant with his general staff 'No offensive biological warfare!' period, end of statement. The very little funding that has been provided for biological warfare is strictly for defensive research, troop protection. Even so, there are no faculties dedicated solely to biological efforts. These efforts are performed mainly at chemical warfare installations. It's true Himmler is very much pro-offensive bio, but he is a minority and does not have Hitler's support. He doesn't even have the full support of his closest associates. Colonels Brandt and Klumm have both spoken out against it.[22] So I can't see Himmler or anybody else starting any major biological program, especially one of the magnitude Gottfried had proposed. Even if Gotffried were still alive, I doubt it would have gotten the support to be implemented. Too many people in high places are against it. Gottfried was a rogue.

"Even so, I can't stand here and tell you Gottfried couldn't have eventually convinced the high command to fund his program. I can't tell you somebody else in the future won't or that the inmates of Staglag 13 will never be subjected to the inhumane experiments Gottfried proposed. I can tell you this: I don't think it's likely to happen, not in the near future anyway. Whether or not the risk warrants evacuation of the camp, that's a decision you are better qualified to make than I. Just be aware, whatever decision you make, you'll have my full support."

There was a knock on the door announcing Carter's entrance.

"'Scuse me sirs, but Kinch just made contact with London. They are sending a plane tomorrow night to pick up Lang and the notebook. They want agent Anders to take possession of the notebook and accompany him."

"Ok," Hogan replied, letting out a breath he wasn't aware he had been holding, "Acknowledge orders. Tell London they'll be there, all three."

"Three, sir?"

"Yeah, Lang, Anders, and the notebook."

"Oh! Right, sir!"

"I can stay if you like. As long as London gets the book, I suspect they could care less what Lang or I do," Mike said as Carter left to relay Hogan's order to Kinch in the radio room.

"Stay and do what?"

"Help you evacuate camp."

"Who said I was going to evacuate camp?" Hogan responded with a twinkle in his eye.

"You did! A few minutes ago."

"No, I said I needed a plan," Hogan corrected. "I didn't say I was going to do it."

"So you are going to stay?"

"Like you said, the odds of anybody implementing a plan of the magnitude of Gottfried's in the near future is pretty small. There is no use in bailing out if we don't have to. Besides," the twinkle in Hogan's eyes broadened into a mischievous gleam, "Now that we know the plan, if we stay we can do something if they do decide to implement it."

Now, that was the Robert Mike had known most of his life — think big and never admit defeat. Maybe that was why he was so successful. Maybe that was why Mike had always liked him.

"There's a farm on the Hammelburg road with a couple nice horses. It's only 2400; the guys will be going to bed soon. Wanna race?"

Mike met Hogan's impish grin with one of his own. It had been a long time since he had raced horses, a LONG time.

Hogan and Anders spent most of the next day squirreled away in Hogan's office. Every so often the sounds of laughter would break through into the common room.

"Now, what do you suppose is going on in there?" Newkirk inquired, nodding toward Hogan's area.

"Top level strategy meeting?" suggested Carter.

"Nah, too much laughing. Strategy meetings are boring," LeBeau explained.

"How do you know? Have you ever been to one?"

"That's why it's called a meeting, because it's boring. If it was fun it would be called a party," Newkirk chimed in.

As darkness descended upon the camp, its permanent occupants began saying good-bye to their guests. Schell was the first to go.

"Doctor," Anders spoke first. "Thanks for everything."

"Yes, thank you very much," echoed Lang.

"I was glad I could be of help."

"If you are ever in this area again, look us up. We're in the yellow pages under 'twenty-four hours service'," Newkirk quipped.

"But, leave the pufferfish at home," added Hogan.

Schell laughed, "Gladly. It's been a pleasure working with you men. Although I must admit, I wish it could have been under different circumstances. I hope my knowledge of pufferfish poison never has to be used this way again."

"I'll buy that! Doc, thanks again. LeBeau, take him out," Hogan ordered.

"Auf Wiedersehen," Schell replied.

A chorus of good-byes followed Schell as he and LeBeau went out the tunnel.

The next checkouts from the Stalag 13 hotel were Anders and Lang.

"Thank you, Colonel Hogan for getting me out of Germany and saving my life."

"Well, as best as I recall, you saved my life also, so I guess that makes us even. Besides, some of the information in that notebook will be very useful to London."

"I just hope someday to be able to return to a Germany like I remember from my childhood."

"That's what we all hope," responded Anders.

"Germany was not always what it is now. Not all Germans are like the Nazis. Most are basically good people. They have been misguided." *Just like me.*

For Hogan's men, saying good-bye to Anders was especially hard. In the few days he had been in camp, he had become like one of the family. By saving Colonel Hogan's life, he had definitely saved their operation, quite possibly saving each of their lives and who knows how many more.

"Colonel, you've got a good group of men here. Men, I've enjoyed working with you. Keep up the good work." Mike shook each man's hand. "Take care of that old mule there," Mike said nodding at Hogan. Hogan's response was a dirty look to end all dirty looks. "So I don't have to come back. I know he has nine lives, but I don't want to make a career out of saving him in each of them."

"Don't worry, we will," replied Kinch, "but you are more than welcome anytime. You don't need a reason."

"Just leave your Nazis turncoat buddies in Berlin where we can bomb them. I have better things to do with my time than to deal with your traitors," quipped Hogan.

Mike grinned.

"Ok, Carter, Newkirk escort Lang and Anders to their plane.

"This way, gents."

Midway up the ladder Mike stopped and yelled, "Oh, Hogan," Hogan looked at him. "Take care of my bike!"

This time it was Hogan's turn to grin.

"My bike."

"Flip you for it after the war," Mike said and hastily exited the tunnel before Hogan could retort.

Kinch gave Hogan a puzzled look. "What was that all about?"

"Private joke," Hogan replied climbing the ladder into the barracks. There was still one loose end he had to tie up.

Kinch contemplated the comment. From the moment Hogan had begun to come out from under the influence of the poison, he and Anders had hit it off amazingly well.

Almost like they had known each other all their lives. Hmm!

Why shouldn't they hit it off, the colonel was a likeable person and so was Anders.

Person! Kinch realized this was the first time since he had known Hogan that he had thought of him in terms of being a person as opposed to being an officer or "the colonel." Kinch wondered what the colonel's life was really like. As the senior allied officer in the area, Hogan shouldered the responsibility for the coordination of all the underground activity in the area as well as for his own unit. As senior officer of the camp, he was responsible for the well being of every man in the camp. It was a delicate balancing act, one Hogan performed admirably well without the benefit of a second-in-command. Kinch and the other guys worked hard and they accomplished a lot, but basically they followed orders. It was Hogan on whose shoulders it fell to give the orders and come up with the ideas. It was Hogan on whom the Nazis focused their attention when they had suspicions. It was Hogan and Hogan alone. And as this latest experience had taught Kinch, the consequences of a mistake or an error in judgement on his part could be dire.

For Robert Hogan the human being, life with those kinds of responsibilities had to be tough. Kinch couldn't understand how the colonel held up because he knew he couldn't. Outside of Klink and Crittendon (who really didn't count because Klink was the enemy and Crittendon was just another problem), Anders was the first person to come through camp anywhere near Hogan's rank or intelligence. He was the first person to whom Hogan could be a person and not an officer. The first person the colonel could relate to as a human being. Kinch could and would do anything he could to make the colonel's life easier, to help him, but he neither could make the decisions nor could he help shoulder the responsibility. Worst of all, the rank barrier prevented him from being what the colonel needed most — a friend. Kinch hoped that someday, somebody a little less transient would come to camp who could fill the friendship role. In the meantime, Kinch made a promise to himself to take a page from Tiptoe's book and pray everyday, not only for himself, but also for the colonel and the other guys — but especially for the colonel.

CHAPTER 6
Reflections

Stalag 13 was a busy place in the days that followed. After Anders had left, Hogan had spent the remainder of the night devising an evacuation plan. He had his men make records of operating procedures and for the entire operation to be kept at a safe place (easily accessible and easily transportable). He instructed the men when and where to plant explosives to bring the entire tunnel structure down, thereby destroying all evidence of their activities. Since most of the camp was involved with the Living Christmas Tree in some form or another, Hogan used Tree practices as a cover to brief his barrack leaders. Tiptoe wasn't happy about having to share his rehearsal time, but given the recent series of events he understood the necessity. Hogan ran drills day in and day out until the operation could be folded and the entire camp evacuated at the drop of a pin. This time he was leaving nothing to chance.

When his men weren't involved in setting up Hogan's evacuation plan, they were occupied with the Living Christmas Tree. Even Hogan himself had been drafted into reading narration.

"I need someone with a commanding presence and a voice of authority," Tiptoe had said. "Besides, you have such a nice voice; it's clear with just a touch of New England accent. Where did you pick that up anyway? I thought you were from Ohio."

Tiptoe's con job was fairly obvious, but since Hogan had no objection he played along. Tiptoe's ear was amazing. It was true Hogan had been born and lived most of his life in Cleveland, but for a brief time his family had lived in Bridgeport, Connecticut when he was a small boy. Apparently, just long enough to pick up a slight accent. Funny, no one had noticed it before.

"Oh, and by the way, wear your dress uniform with the decorations and all the impressive stuff. It will give the performance a touch of class."

Hogan resisted the urge to remind Tiptoe that he wasn't playing colonel anymore. However, Hogan realized it was Tiptoe's program. The private knew what he wanted to accomplish, whether anyone else did or not, and he needed a certain amount of authority and support from Hogan to achieve his goals. For that reason, Hogan decided to cut him some slack. It wouldn't kill Hogan to wear a tie. Besides, Helga, the Kommandant''s secretary, was coming. Maybe if he played his cards right, afterward they could sneak out to the motor pool and celebrate Christmas in the back of Klink's staff car.

"So, when do you need me for rehearsal?"

"Christmas Eve."

"Did you say 'Christmas Eve'?" Hogan repeated not certain he had heard correctly.

"Yeah, we'll go all the way through it once to see how it falls together."

Hogan shook his head in amazement and walked away. Hogan had a reputation for being somewhat haphazardous, but even for him this was too much.

Hogan had all but forgotten about the Living Christmas Tree when, two days before Christmas, Tiptoe walked into his office with scribbled notes on a sheet of paper.

"What's this?" a puzzled Hogan asked.

"Narration for the Tree. You said you would do it, remember?"

"How can I read narration when I can't read it?" Hogan exclaimed trying to decipher Tiptoe's handwriting and giving up. Tiptoe should have been a doctor.

"And what's this?!" Hogan asked pointing to a sheet of paper that vaguely resembled a list.

"It's the program. So you know when the narrator chimes in."

"I've never heard of Hal Cho." It sounded like a Chinese American, but Hogan didn't remember any Chinese Americans in camp.

"Is this a new prisoner or some new code?"

"That's short for the *Hallelujah Chorus.*"

"The *Hallelujah Chorus,*" Hogan repeated in disbelief, "Do you think you can write this out so I can read it?"

"Probably not."

"Well, do you think you can at least decode the program? And Private, that's not a request."

"Yes, sir."

A short time later Tiptoe returned with a list that at least resembled a program. A few of the items were actually legible. Since Kinch was heavily involved in setting up the record keeping part of Hogan's evacuation plan, Hogan sweet-talked Helga into typing up Tiptoe's scribbles so Hogan could read them. At first Helga looked at the notes, then at Hogan like he had lost his mind. For three pounds of coffee, five pair of nylons, and an untold number of kisses — well, that part, at least, was fun — the blond haired, blue-eyed beauty agreed to do it.

December 25, 1942
Stalag 13

It was a crisp winter's day; a blanket of fresh snow covered the ground. The whole area looked like a giant Christmas card, that is, if you ignored the barbed wire fences, the towers, and the armed guards. Despite the reminders of the war, excitement filled the air. Today was the first annual Stalag 13 Living Christmas Tree. Hogan hoped by next Christmas the war would be over, making this the first and last Stalag 13 Living Christmas Tree.

The recreation hall was packed. Klink, Helga, Schultz, and most of the off-duty German personnel in camp had come to see what all the excitement was about. All the prisoners who weren't actively participating in the production were seated facing a make-shift stage with drawn curtains. Hogan had to admit he was more than a little curious himself. All week long all the men in camp had been whispering and giggling like kids trying to keep a secret from mom. Even during the one rehearsal Hogan was required to attend as narrator, he had not been allowed to see the finished project.

"Top Secret, enlisted men only," Newkirk had told him, with a cocky grin.

Well, if it kept the men active and morale up, who was he to argue. Besides, he had his hands full.

Following some preliminary announcements, Tiptoe took his position at the director's spot center stage. As the curtains opened revealing the long awaited "tree," it took every ounce of discipline Hogan had in him not to laugh at the sight. Over fifty men lined a series of six risers converging to a point just below the ceiling. The bottom tier had 19 men, the next one up had 15men, the third had 10 men, the fourth tier had 6 men, the fifth had 3 men, and the final tier held only one man. Each man wore a robe dyed green made out of old parachutes, burlap sacks, or any other cloth they could get their hands on. On the fronts of the robes they had fastened greenery from evergreen trees sneaked in during a work detail outside the fence. Along with the limbs, they had fastened homemade ornaments. At the very top, standing alone on the top riser was little LeBeau. Unlike the others he was dressed in a white robe complete with wings, a halo, and an angelic (or devilish, Hogan couldn't determine which) expression on his face. All and all, it did resemble a Christmas tree, a squatty Christmas tree, but a Christmas tree nevertheless.

Hogan never ceased to be amazed at the ingenuity his men displayed when they set their minds to something. They could almost win the war by themselves. They were indeed a good group of men. No, they were better than good, they were extraordinary in their dedication and in their sacrifice. Most of them stayed in this rotten camp month after month because Hogan asked them to — for the benefit of fellow soldiers whom they would never know. And when Hogan himself had fallen into Gestapo hands, when by all rights they should have been out of the tunnels and back in England, they still stayed. They stayed and almost literally brought him back from hell. To Hogan they were the cream of the crop, and he was proud to be their commander.

The men under Hogan's command loved him in return. They hoped to make him forget the war for just a few minutes, especially that close call a couple of weeks ago. The whole affair had been a rude awakening as to the value of a good commander; their colonel was the best. The expression on Hogan's face as he saw the tree for the first time was the best pay off in the world. The equally astounded expressions of their fellow inmates was icing on the cake. Somehow it made all the hard work seem worthwhile. The radiant countenance of the men in the production lit the room better than any source of artificial lighting could. As Tiptoe raised his arms and began to direct, the majestic sounds of a four-part harmony rang throughout the building:

> Hallelujah!　Hallelujah!　Hallelujah!　Hallelujah!
> Hallelujah!
> Hallelujah!　Hallelujah!　Hallelujah!　Hallelujah!
> Hallelujah!
> For the Lord God Omnipotent reigneth.
> Hallelujah! Hallelujah! Hallelujah! Hallelujah…

Here each of the four parts broke way and sang not only different notes, but also different phases. *Some of the notes still aren't quite right, and we won't discuss the timing,* Hogan observed. But it didn't matter, the song had a pleasant sound and, more importantly, it came from the heart:

> …and he shall reign forever and ever,
> King of Kings, and Lord of Lords.
> Hallelujah!　Hallelujah!　Hallelujah!　Hallelujah!
> Hallelujah! [23]

Not more than a few weeks ago the existence of an omnipotent being controlling the entire universe was a concept Hogan would have laughed at despite having attended church as a child. If asked, he would have claimed that each person made his own way in the world. But the events of the past few weeks were forcing him to rethink his views. It wasn't so much the events themselves, but the timing. Events like

Timothy/Mike coming back into his life after all these years (and of all things) as an OSS agent just when the camp —when *he* — needed someone with espionage expertise and leadership abilities, and Gottfried being called away to investigate a fire during Hogan's interrogation which gave Anders and his men time to plan the rescue before Gottfried had the chance to torture him. The oddest of all was the calming affect Tiptoe's prayers had on him when the paralysis of Schell's poison activated his claustrophobia with its massive panic attacks. The timing on all these events was just plain spooky.

As the song ended and the next began, Hogan focused his attention back on the tree.

I heard the bells on Christmas Day. Their old familiar carols play.
And wild and sweet the words repeat of peace on earth good will to men.
And in despair I bowed my head: 'There is no peace on earth,' I said 'For hate is strong and mocks the song of peace on earth good will to men.'

Maybe there were no bells in camp, but the sound of men singing carols was a beautiful sound. It was a sound that only a couple of weeks ago had been marred by despair. Despair — an emotion the camp certainly had seen plenty of during the days of Hogan's capture and incapacitation. Every man in camp had lived with the knowledge that if the Gestapo uncovered their operation, the entire camp would suffer the consequences. With that knowledge, there had been little hope and little peace, only fear which bred hatred. Hatred for the Gestapo and for the Nazis. Hatred that made everything and everybody an enemy. Hatred that threatened to turn the men of camp into the very kind of being they were fighting. Hatred that choked all feelings of peace and good will.

> Then peeled the bells more loud and deep: God is not dead,
> Nor doth he sleep; the wrong shall fail the right prevail,
> With peace on earth, good will to men... [24]

Just when it had seemed things were at their darkest and there was no place to turn, along had come an OSS agent and a doctor, both of German heritage — the enemy. And yet, the two had risked their lives to free Hogan from the Gestapo and they had succeeded!

While Goldilocks died in a cold dark cell in Cologne, his death brought life to Papa Bear. Similarly, years before Timothy Sonntag had died to give birth to Mike Anders. Both were born with a drive and spirit that knew no bounds. For as long as men like Papa Bear and Anders existed, men willing to take a stand and determined to show the Nazis that the world won't tolerate brutal behavior, then there was hope that could make a difference. Hope that eventually right *would* prevail.

The song was ending and that was Hogan's cue. Hogan walked up to the podium and began to read:

> And there were in the same country shepherds abiding in the field, keeping watch over their flock by night. And lo, the angel of the Lord came upon them, and the glory of the Lord shown round about them: and they were sore afraid. And the angel said unto them, Fear not: for, behold I bring you good tidings of great joy, which shall be to all people. For unto you

is born this day in the city of David a Savior, which is Christ the Lord. And this *shall* be a sign unto you; ye shall find the babe wrapped in swaddling clothes, lying in a manger. And suddenly there was with the angel a multitude of the heavenly host praising God and saying, Glory to God in the highest, and on earth peace good will toward men.[25]

Peace would come, but not for another two and a half years, and the price would be steep. During the war a total of 47 million people in the European theater would lose their lives, 29 million of which were civilians. Some like Greta and Anne Henderson had the misfortune of being in the wrong place at the wrong time. Others had the wrong ethic background. And many died fighting for a world without fear of tyranny or oppression, fighting for freedom.

For the survivors, life would never be the same. For many, the bombs, the guns, and the desolate conditions would leave permanent trauma. Peace would bring a time of joy and rebuilding, but it would also bring a time of decision. A decision, which must be made by nations and individuals alike. To decide whether to let the ugliness of the war they had just experienced consume them — to live in bitterness, hatred, anger, and self destruction — or to learn the lessons of life and experience the richness of growth that comes from perseverance through hardship, and the inner peace of forgiving. To leave the past in the past and get on with living. For a war-ravaged world, peace would truly bring a time for new beginnings.

(ENDNOTES)

[1] Biological Warfare
[2] Special Intelligence Service
[3] *Monkey Business*
[4] Military slang for "biological"
[5] Articles of the Geneva Convention 1929
[6] *Hold That Tiger*
[7] *Psychic Kommandant*
[8] German for "Protective Echelon"
[9] 1 Samuel 3
[10] The Institute of Entomology of the Waffen SS and Police was established in 1942 for the control of rats, fleas, and other insects as well as biological warfare research (*SIPRI Chemical and Biological Warfare Studies. Vol 18. Biological and Toxic Weapons and Use from the Middle Ages to 1945.* Oxford Press. 1999).
[11] The Treaty of Versailles, signed in 1919, set up a reparations committee that would meet in May of 1921 to determine the reparations the Germans would have to pay for World War I. Until then, Germany would have to payback $5,000,000,000, almost half of which was paid by 1921. The ruling of the reparations committee was that Germany should pay an additional $25,000,000,000. In 1918 the total sum of money in the German Reichbank was $577,089,500.
[12] Woodrow Wilson proposed a settlement in which he called the "14 points." In these, Germany would retain most of its pre-war territory and pay little or no reparations. He was overruled.
[13] *The Great Impersonation*
[14] *A Bad Day in Berlin*
[15] Until his assassination, Reinhard Heydrich, was second-in-

command to Himmler within the SS. He was noted as being a very brilliant but cruel leader.

[16] *Reservations Are Required*

[17] *Operation Briefcase*

[18] *Physics,* Third Edition, David Halliday and Robert Resnick , John Wiley and Sons, 1978, p 151

[19] Roosevelt signed a lend-lease agreement providing material and personnel to England in March 1941.

[20] It still is today. According to William Haugan Light (Eye of Newt, Skin of Toad, Bile of Pufferfish, 1998) between 100 and 200 people become seriously intoxicated each year, half of which result in fatalities even with treatment.

[21] Assassins shot Reinhard Heydrich, on 27 May 1942. He died on 4 June 1942. Himmler did not replace Heydrich until 30 January 1943.

[22] *SIPRI Chemical and Biological Warfare Studies. Vol 18. Biological and Toxic Weapons Use from the Middle Ages to 1945.* Oxford Press. 1999

[23] "The Hallelujah Chorus," from *The Messiah* by G.F Handel. Copyright 1912 by G. Schimmer, Inc.

[24] Henry W. Longfellow

[25] Luke 2:8-14. The King James' version.